I0722218

I've included two books in one. The first,

Is the book you have been waiting for *The Other Side of Privileged. The second is   Orlana, The Golden Faery Queen*, which is a children's book that my main character in (Zoey) references. Her life mirrors Orlana's, and so I felt it was appropriate to include both. I hope you enjoy.

Sheri Chapman

The Other Side of Privileged

By Sheri Chapman

Edited by Susette at My Write Hand VA

Cover by Veronique Poirier

<u>CHAPTERS</u>

Prologue

AGE FIVE

"Daddy, can we watch Orlana, the Golden Faery Queen again?" I asked.

"No, baby, not tonight," Daddy said, scooping me up. "I'll read you the story before bedtime, though."

I squealed as he spun me in a circle.

"Thank you, darling," Mommy said to my father. "I'm so burned out right now. I just can't do it today," she laughed.

"Once a kid gets a story they love, they do wear it out," Daddy said. He turned to me. "Go get washed up for bed and brush your teeth. Then hop in bed. I'll be there in a minute to read to you."

I giggled. "Okay, Daddy."

Daddy threw my toddler brother in the air then tucked him in his arms and carried Brycen to his room. Mommy took me to get ready for bed.

"There you go, my beautiful princess," Mommy said. She patted my mouth dry after I rinsed. "You know I love you so much."

"Mommy?" I looked up at her.

"Yes, darling?"

"Are you *really* tired of Orlana, the Golden Faery Queen?"

She smiled and patted my leg. "No, honey. I just needed a break from reading that story tonight. I'm sure I'll want to read it to you at least five times tomorrow."

I grinned. "Really?

"Really."

"Oh, thank you, Mommy." I wrapped my arms around her neck and hugged her tight. She carried me to my room and put me in bed. She covered my feet and folded back the blanket at my waist.

"Does someone in here want me to read a story?" Daddy asked, peeking in the room.

I raised my arm and wiggled my hand real hard. "I do, Daddy, I do!"

"Calm down, young lady," he laughed. He sat on the edge of my bed. "I'll read it to you."

Daddy held a book with a golden cover that showed a beautiful fairy fluttering across the expanse. She had blonde hair and very blue eyes. Her wings were colored like a Monarch's, and they had a glittery sheen that made them sparkle in the sun. A crown of glittery diamonds was atop her head, and she held a similar wand in her hand.

"She's so pretty, Daddy," I said, pointing to the cover.

"Not as pretty as you are," Daddy said, tickling me.

I giggled then laughed, squirming under his large fingers.

When I could catch my breath, I said, "Please read it, Daddy."

Daddy opened the cover and began to read.

My Idol

AGE EIGHT

The sun cooked the top of my head as we pushed through the sweltering hotness. I didn't care, though. I was having the time of my life. My hand was swallowed up by my daddy's, and Mama tagged behind with my brother in tow. I was eight, and Brycen was five.

"Mommy, look!" I shouted, pointing. "It's Orlana, the Golden Faery Queen! And she has a carriage."

"And it's even in the brightest part of the day," Daddy added. Smile lines crinkled in the corners of his eyes.

A parade of Faery Tale Land characters was making its way toward us. People surged forward making it nearly impossible for me to see through the wall of humanity. I squealed in delight as Daddy hoisted me up on his broad shoulders.

"Hang on, Princess," he instructed as he stooped down to also raise my brother. Mama was busy snapping pictures of us on Daddy and of the fairy princess and dancers around the carriage.

"This is *sooooo wonderful*!" I exclaimed in awe. My voice definitely sounded as moon-struck as I felt. Orlana was my favorite story *ever*.

My attention never wavered from the gorgeous young woman singing and dancing in her carriage. Her ice-lavender dress shimmered elegantly against her Monarch wings as the character swirled and waved to her fans. A brilliant tiara of diamonds winked at me from a distance.

Finally, the procession paused. My idol got out of the vehicle and staged a performance directly in front of us. When she began to move on, Daddy deposited us with Mama.

"Give me a second," he said.

I watched the dark-haired figure of my father move toward the woman in the shimmery lavender dress. When there was a lull in the music, Daddy approached Orlana. The blonde turned her head to greet and smile at him.

The sun trapped in her hair reflected spun gold. Orlana seemed to listen intently then nodded in response to something Daddy said. A million diamonds twinkled from her tiara with the movement.

Beaming, my father turned toward us and motioned enthusiastically for us to come.

"I think your father wants us to go over there," Mama whispered dramatically in my ear.

"Really?" I squealed.

Through her warm amusement, Mama said, "Really."

In my excitement, I raced toward my dad as fast as I could without looking back. The people teeming in front of me let me pass with relative ease. It seemed like forever, but we were by my father's side at last.

"Young lady, you wait for your mother next time," Daddy admonished me. He tried to look serious, but I could see traces of amusement twitching behind his lips.

"Yes, Daddy," I said, contrite.

I could feel my eyes widen as I peeked up at the woman standing next to my father.

"Hello, young lady," she said in a musical voice. Her eyes were baby blue and were highlighted by the sheen of her gown.

"H – hi," I stuttered.

"I hear it's a very special day for you." Her golden Monarch wings glowed from behind her.

"Yes, ma'am," I breathed. "I get to meet YOU!"

Orlana beamed at me. Then she straightened and announced to the audience, "Everyone, today is this young lady's birthday. What's your name, sweetie?"

"Zoey Lovette," I managed.

"How old are you, Zoey?" Her voice was pure melody.

"I'm eight today," I announced proudly. I could feel my chest puff up slightly.

The beautiful princess smiled brightly and addressed the crowd.

"Let's all wish Zoey a happy eighth birthday," Orlana suggested.

The crowd mirrored her proposal and collectively wished me a happy birthday.

I was so pleased. Not only did I get to meet my favorite fairy tale princess, but she wished me a happy birthday, too.

"In addition," came the perfect and cultured voice, "I have something for you."

"You... do?" I gulped.

"Yes, my dear." Orlana went back to her carriage and retrieved something. She held it behind her back before presenting it to me.

"I'd like to give you a wand," she said. The blonde pushed a silver baton into my hand. It was slender, about a foot and a half long. It ended in a star shape that sparkled with little diamonds. They twinkled and winked at me as I admired them.

I looked up at Orlana and breathed, "Th – thank you!" I couldn't manage more than that.

She squatted a little so that she was on my level. "You're very welcome. Have a great day." Then she dazzled me more with a radiant smile that was just for me.

"It's the best, E.V.E.R," I whispered. Then, she made my world because she gave me a quick hug.

I was a chatterbox for nearly an hour after Orlana's departure. I remember sitting in the shade with a hamburger and a soda full of crushed ice. It was the hottest part of the day, and we were wilting.

"Daddy, can we get some Dippin Dots and then ride The Faery Hills Rollercoaster?" I asked.

"You bet, baby," he said as he ruffled my silky blonde hair.

"Honey," Mama said, "I think I'll take Brycen and do some smaller scale rides while you two stand in line."

"Okay. I'll text you when we finish."

"Sounds good," Mama said.

Mama had blonde hair, kind of like Orlana's, but Mama's was a darker honey color. Her eyes were emerald green instead of blue, but she was still beautiful.

Daddy and I purchased the Dipping Dots and sat to eat our ice cream while Mama wandered away with my brother. Right before we approached The Faery Hills Rollercoaster, Daddy asked me if I needed to go to the bathroom.

"Yes, I do."

"I do, too. It won't take me long. I'll be right out here by that bench. Do *not* go anywhere without me." His hazel eyes bored into mine.

"Yes, Daddy."

There were lines everywhere in Faery Tale Land, even in the bathroom. I still had my wand gripped tightly in my hand. While I waited, I stared at it. It was my most prized possession.

"Hi, Zoey," a bigger woman greeted me. Not only was she taller than Mama, but she was also thickly made. She had plain brown hair in a bun on the back of her neck, and she wore a dress that looked a lot like a sheet of material with arm and neck holes. The fabric was a base color of light green with a pattern of palm trees, and it clung to her generous curves.

I looked around a bit, not sure if she was speaking to me. The woman looked at me. Her brown eyes stared directly into my blue ones.

"I saw you out there. It was pretty neat that Orlana gave you that nice-looking wand."

"Oh, yeah," I said, holding my cherished trophy a little higher so she could see it better.

"It would go really well with a dress I bought my granddaughter," she mused.

"Really?" It was hard to contain my excitement.

The woman slipped her thick hand into her package and pulled out a silky lavender dress that glimmered in the light.

"*Oooohhhh*," I breathed. "It's so pretty!"My eyes had to be silver dollars with my amazement at the garment.

"You know," the woman said thoughtfully. "You look about the same size as my granddaughter. Do you want to try it on?"

"Oh, could I?" I squealed. I tried not to dance with excitement, but I knew I wasn't successful when I saw the woman's amused smile.

"Just don't get it dirty," she said.

I could scarcely wait to try on the beautiful dress. I hung it carefully on the hook until I could use the facility. Then I took my clothes off and neatly folded them. I slipped the cool fabric onto my damp skin. I wouldn't be able to zip it without assistance.

I looked for her when I exited the stall. The woman was standing closer than I expected.

She said, "Oh, *my*! Don't you make a pretty picture?"

"Could you zip me up?" I asked shyly.

I presented my back to her and felt the dress tighten appropriately on my body.

"This dress was made for you," the woman said with an approving nod. Her dull-brown eyes appraised me.

I didn't know how to answer that.

"Do you want to show your daddy?" She arched a brow and smiled again. She seemed very friendly.

"Oh, could I?" I asked. I couldn't refrain from bouncing on my toes.

"Of course," she said. "But let's surprise him, okay?"

"How?" I asked and stilled my movement as I awaited her answer.

She pulled a blanket out of another package. She said in a conspirator's whisper, "I'll wrap you in this until we get in front of him so he can't see you too soon. Then, I'll take the blanket off your head, and he'll see you all at one time."

"Okay! My daddy will be so proud!" I said.

The woman put the blanket over my head and guided me out of the bathroom. I felt disoriented, so I wasn't concerned when we seemed to be going in the wrong direction.

We'd walked for a few minutes before I said, "Is he there? We should be there by now."

"I see him just over here. *Wait*," she whispered, "Don't look yet! We don't want to spoil the surprise."

I shuffled further. Finally, I complained, "It's too hot in here. I don't care if he sees now."

The woman said, "Okay, I want you to sit on this bench for a second while I take the blanket off. We want the dress to be pretty and not wrinkled."

"Okay."

The woman took the covering off, and I sat on the bench. She made a small production of arranging the dress around me. Finally, she took out a cloth from another bag.

"Why do you have that rag in a baggie?" I asked. "And where is my daddy?"

"I told him to come in just a minute.   This rag has Orlana perfume on it.   Do you want to smell?"
"Yes, please."

Training Begins

HOURS LATER:

I awoke in the back of a cramped car. I blinked groggily a few times. I was trying to figure out where I was. *Did I fall asleep and Daddy bring me here to wait for Mama and Brycen?*

The vibration of traveling combined with the after effects of the chemicals on the cloth made me feel ill. I tried to sit up but a wave of nausea threatened to consume me. I collapsed back and closed my eyes to reduce the effects of the dizzy spell.

"It looks like the little lady is comin' around," said a male voice.

"Should be about that time," came the semi-familiar voice of my abductee.

I smacked my mouth a few times before rasping, "Wh – where am I?"

The man was as thin as the woman was heavy. He had greasy black hair and squinty eyes. Reddish-brown freckles crowded his face.

He laughed deep in his throat and said, "You're in the back of a car, genius."

My heart started beating faster. This didn't seem like a very nice man. I shook off the last remnants of sleepiness and was truly afraid for the first time in my sheltered life.

"Where's my mama and daddy?" I whispered.

"Well, they ain't here, sweetheart," he said with a wink. "You belong to us now."

I bolted upright. I looked around wildly, but there wasn't much to see. It looked like we were driving through swampy-looking land with some palm trees scattered close to the road.

"Do you like the Everglades?" the man asked with a grin splitting his face. "Where we're going, you really won't want to go exploring unless you like to pet alligators."

My heart was pumping madly in my chest and my throat threatened to gag me with the sudden lump. I could feel tears well up in my eyes.

"Oh, the widdle baby is gonna cry," the man mimicked. He rubbed his eyes with his fists in a mocking gesture.

"Leave her be," the woman said gruffly. "Give her time to adjust. It's hard when they first realize."

"I was just having fun, Sally," the man said grumpily.

"There'll be plenty of time for that during her training," Sally said.

The man slouched back in his seat and folded his arms across his chest. He didn't say anything more to me for the rest of the ride.

I stared out the window and silently cried. I couldn't stop the multitude of thoughts from crowding in my head, but I was sure there would be no forthcoming answers.

What had I done? What was going to happen to me? Where were Mama, Daddy, and Brycen? Most importantly: were they okay?

We probably traveled a couple of hours more before veering down a very secluded road. I never would've noticed it if the car hadn't suddenly turned. It seemed like another twenty minutes passed before we finally pulled up to an older looking home. A dated model blue suburban sat in the drive.

An airboat was in the back. It was tied to a short dock made with boards that had seen better days. The place was surrounded by a boggy swamp. Cypress trees and other strange plants seemed to congregate around the structure.

"Welcome to your new home," the man said. "Well, for the next six months or so."

"Why am I here?" I suddenly blurted out. "What do you want with me?"

When no one answered, I leaned forward. My fingers clutched the seat tightly in my panic.

"Please, take me home! My daddy will give you money."

"Awww, her daddy will give us money. Did you hear that, Sally?" The man sneered. "Just what do you think you're worth, darlin'? Ten dollars?"

Sally turned to look at me and said, "Zoey, I'm in the market for children. I won't sell you back to your parents because I'll go to jail, but you *will* be sold to the highest bidder. If you shut up and follow the rules, you can have a decent time here. Do you understand?"

I looked at her and nodded glumly. I really didn't understand what she was telling me, but I did understand how I felt: helpless and trapped. I wanted to run when the back door opened, but I realized that would be futile. The man would catch me and then they'd purposefully make me more miserable.

Sally led the way to the house. I followed her, and the man trailed in my wake. She opened the door and then led me to a little room with no windows. There was a single mattress in the corner covered with a clean sheet, a small traveling pillow, and a blanket.

"Home, sweet home," crooned the man.

"Zoey, this is Nick," Sally said. Before I could respond, she ordered, "Nick, go check on the others."

Once he was gone, I asked quietly, "Sally, why did you take me?"

"Because you have blonde hair and blue eyes. You're a pretty little thing, and you'll sell well. I just hope you're a quick learner. I don't want to have to get rough with you." She waited to see the effect her words had on me.

I sank into the mattress. I could feel the tears bubbling up again.

"You have yourself a good little cry. Then it'll be time to eat and get ready for bed. You'll start training in the morning," Sally said unsympathetically. "There's a roll of toilet paper in the corner if you need to blow your nose."

Sally left and shut the door gently behind her. I didn't need to be told that the door was locked because I heard the key turning. I buried my face in the pillow and let the misery surround me. Soon, it began pouring out. When my jailer finally returned, I was completely spent.

"Time to eat," she said.

"I'm not hungry," I stated dispassionately.

"You'll need your strength for tomorrow," she advised. "I won't make you eat, but I highly recommend it."

I slowly got up. I wanted to get out of this room, so I decided to try to eat a few bites. I followed Sally to the kitchen. Nick was there with a young woman with light brown hair and gray eyes.

She appeared to be an older girl but an adult by my eight-year-old standards. Her shoulders slumped, and she avoided direct eye contact. She had a way of shrinking back that made her easy to overlook. This girl waited on the two adults hand and foot.

Also seated at the table were three other children. There was a boy with midnight hair and olive skin. He was about six. The other two were girls about my age or just a little younger. One had hair a beautiful shade of auburn, and the other had dark hair that complimented her dark, heavily-fringed eyes.

I smiled at them. Before I could get a word out, I was interrupted.

"NO talking allowed," Nick stated firmly. "You'll do your work. No need to communicate other than to ask one of us adults for directions if you need help."

Nick snapped his fingers and pointed to the glasses. The young woman got up and filled them with water for us. Sally went to the fridge and retrieved bologna sandwiches with American cheese that were packaged in baggies. She sat down heavily then tossed each of us the meal. There were no condiments on the bread.

"Eat up," she said.

Everyone seemed to be looking at me. It was as if they thought I'd complain about the fare, but I was too overwhelmed and scared to say much of anything. I meekly took a bite of the dull sandwich. I chewed slowly, hoping my saliva glands would moisten the dry bread soon so that I could swallow it.

I ended up eating about half of the sandwich and drank all my water.

Shortly after, Sally stood and said, "Jez, you clean the kitchen with Lucinda. Javier, you can clean the floors in here, and I do mean it better be a notable improvement over the last time, and Deidra, you can sweep the rest of the house. Lucinda will tell me if you don't do a good job. Zoey, I'll see you to the bathroom and then bed. You're done for the night."

The next morning, I awoke early. No one was up yet, but I could feel the damp morning pressing in on me. I'd had dreams about alligators snapping down on hands holding spoons of Dipping Dots and pretty Orlana princesses dancing around and laughing at my daddy. The dreams disturbed me nearly as much as my waking reality until I became fully aware. Then, the terror of my present situation sunk in.

It wasn't long before the key turned in the lock. Sally was there with a small smile.

"Rise and shine," she said. "Go get washed up, and then come to the kitchen."

I did as I was told. When I walked in the room, Sally informed me that I was going to start with food preparation. After weeks of learning how to prepare meals, then she'd teach me how to deep clean.

"You see," Sally informed me, "I already have a buyer for you. They want you to basically be a maid for them." She paused then added thoughtfully, "My job now is to make sure you can cook well and you know how to properly clean. I've got a reputation to uphold, and you'll do me proud."

All I could do was stare wide-eyed at her.

"Lucinda, you start her off with easy things, but tell her how to do *every* little thing. She comes from a home that I'm sure hasn't taught her a thing about work."

"Yes, ma'am," the woman said quietly. Her eyes flashed up at Sally to acknowledge her and then dropped quickly to the floor. Her voice was soft-spoken and a little tremulous.

"Go ahead and get started, then," Sally said. "Chop! Chop! I'll get the other kids started on chores while you two cook."

I looked up at Lucinda. I hadn't the foggiest idea of what I was supposed to do. I know she could see the question in my eyes.

"Go to the fridge and get out the carton of eggs and butter," she instructed, "and get the bread out of the cabinet. We'll toast it."

While I grabbed the items. Lucinda turned the heat on under a skillet. I watched as she dripped in some oil and swirled it around the pan.

"This will help keep the eggs from sticking," she explained. "Crack the eggs in a bowl and mix them up really good."

"Okay," I said meekly. At least she was nice and not intimidating.

"You see this setting on the burner?" Lucinda asked, pointing to the large dated dial on the stove.

"Yes," I said.

"You want it to be in the middle, medium heat or so, maybe a little lower, for scrambling the eggs. I'll help you watch them, okay?"

"Thank you," I muttered. My mama always made the eggs for breakfast in my house. My eyes welled in sorrow.

"Don't lose your train of thought," Lucinda instructed. "It's best to stay focused on your work."

I nodded then took the spatula from her. She poured the eggs in the hot skillet. They sizzled and bubbled.

"Keep scraping the spatula through them so they cook in crumbles instead of in sheets," Lucinda advised. "They get too dry if they aren't stirred frequently."

I tried. Some of the eggs stuck, but most of them appeared to crumble. Lucinda told me when they looked done and turned off the stove.

"Move the pan off the hot burner and let's start on the toast," she suggested, "and cover them so they stay hot."

"Okay," I said and performed the chore. Afterwards, I placed two pieces of bread in the toaster and waited until they popped up.

"Now you butter them," Lucinda instructed, "but be careful. The butter isn't softened, and you can rip the bread."

Despite Lucinda's warning, I ripped the toast. Every piece. I really did try, but it was my first time ever touching food that I wasn't going to eat right away.

Ten minutes later, everyone was seated.

"Well, well, well, we really do have a novice," Sally said, holding up a piece of her ripped toast. She tossed it down in disgust. "You'll have to do better next time, Zoey."

I nodded and looked down. At least the eggs looked normal. I felt accomplished because it was my first time cooking them as well. However, Sally never mentioned them. I'd have to take the fact she ate them as success.

Sally turned to Nick. "We got a gator that's causing a bit of mischief close to our dock again."

"Want me to kill it?"

"That's why I'm telling you," Sally said. "We better get rid of him before he gets braver."

My eyes were wide. I couldn't imagine killing an alligator. *Did that mean... they had a gun?* I swallowed hard.

"Zoey, you're going to clean the kitchen. Lucinda, help her. You're her teacher while she's learning kitchen stuff. Make sure she cleans the dishes correctly."

Once she'd left the kitchen, I whispered, "All we do is rinse them off and put them in the dishwasher, right?"

"You won't get to use the dishwasher for a long time, yet," Lucinda whispered back. "Sally makes you learn everything the hard way first. Only after you're an expert will she teach you how to use machines to make cleaning easier."

First, we rinsed all the dishes. Then we placed them in scalding hot soapy water to soak while we wiped down the table and counters. Then Lucinda taught me how to scrub the dishes and rinse them. I had to run a finger over the fronts and backs to make sure every morsel had been removed. If any particle still remained on the plate, it was sent back into the dishwater to rescrub.

Then we dried them until they shone. Just when we finished placing the dinnerware back in their designated places, Sally walked in the room.

"Take a few minutes, and then I want you to polish the silverware," she said. "That's your next chore for the day."

About that time, Nick walked through. He went to the fridge and began rummaging through the contents. When he didn't find anything he wanted, he turned to the freezer. He took out a huge chunk of what turned out to be frozen fish and placed it in our newly polished sink to thaw.

"Don't touch that," he said to us with a nod toward the sink.

Wide-eyed, we both nodded. Both of us stared at the sink. We knew that had to be the lure for the alligator.

"Well, don't just stand there," Sally barked. "Get busy. Lucinda! You know where the rags and polish are."

"Yes, ma'am," she responded with a startled jump.

"Zoey, I expect you both to show respect to your elders," Sally said, crossing her arms over her ample chest.

Lucinda poked my ribs lightly and muttered, "Say what I did."

"Uhm, yes, ma-am," I said.

Sally gave a nod and left the room.

"Come on," Lucinda said. "Let's take the silverware to the table. At least we can sit and do it."

"Okay," I said again. I felt like that was the only thing I could manage to say.

Two hours later, we finally finished. Of course, Sally walked in with perfect timing. It made me feel like the woman was psychic. *Maybe the wall had eyes.* Without meaning to, my eyes scanned the room.

Buttered Bread

"You two take a ten-minute break. Go to the bathroom if you need. Get a drink of water. Then we need to start lunch." Sally paused to stare at us. Her eyes shifted back and forth between Lucinda and me. "Zoey, you need to practice buttering bread. I want you to make grilled cheese. I'm going to be stricter. Every piece of bread you rip, you have to eat. Whether it's one or twenty, you'll eat every one. Only serve the buttered slices that are properly dressed. Do you understand me?"

"Y – yes m – ma'am," I stuttered.

Sally continued, "Lucinda, help her with the cooking part. You know how easily grilled cheeses burn. That is not to be tolerated."

"Yes, ma'am," we both uttered the required response together.

The large woman walked to a cabinet and opened it. She took out two loaves of bread.

"If she runs through these loaves, there are more in the freezer."

Lucinda nodded.

I felt my shoulders slumping as Sally turned to exit the room. Tears were pooling in my eyes.

"Here, honey. Let's sit and rest," Lucinda said sympathetically. Her kindness nearly made me wail.

She poured two glasses of water and brought them to the table. Then she sat beside me.

"I know this is hard," she said. "It's hard not having a friend or even appreciation for what you do right. I wish I could say that you get used to it, but you never do."

"H – how long have you been here?" I asked through the catch in my breath. I wiped my tears.

"I was nine when they grabbed me. I turn twenty in a few weeks," she replied flatly.

I could feel my eyes swallow up my face. Any hope I'd been feeling was suddenly dashed.

"They keep you that long?" I managed.

"Well, I'm the only one that's stayed here. Most get sold shortly after training," Lucinda said.

"Why didn't they sell you?" I asked.

"Probably because I'm easily cowed. They terrify me, so they don't worry about me trying to run. I'm a hard-worker and a good trainer. For the captives I'm assigned to work with, I'm usually able to help them make the transition from freedom into slavery easier," she answered honestly. "You all are the only friends I'll ever have." The edges of her lips quivered, but she didn't let the water enter her eyes.

I reached out a hand to comfort her. She had a tremulous smile for me. However, when a tear leaked from her eye, she brushed it angrily away. It was the first emotion I'd noticed on her aside from fear.

"Come," she said, standing abruptly. "We should use the bathroom before we start on lunch."

This time, buttering the bread was a new challenge. My hope was that it would be a little easier because at least I kind of knew how, but the bread was soft, not toasted, and the hardened spread was just as cold. We weren't allowed to melt the butter in the pan, because according to Sally, we used too much that way, and I "needed the practice".

By the third piece of ripped bread, I began to cry.

"Honey, just take your time. Do it like this."

Lucinda took the bread from my hand. With a butter knife, she scraped a tiny shaving onto the front part of the utensil. After several passes, she wiped it gently over the surface of the slice.

Lucinda said, "It may take a lot longer, but you won't rip the bread as easily." Her gray eyes had kindness in their depths, and a look of understanding passed between us.

I took a slow but deep breath and stopped crying. I sniffed as I took the knife from her and tried myself. I ended up ripping two more, but finally, I'd figured it out.

The smell of grilled sandwiches began to fill the house. It wasn't long before Sally came to check on us.

"Zoey, set the table while Lucinda finishes up. Put one piece of cheese on your plate and those ripped slices of bread."

I nodded. I turned quickly so she wouldn't see my chin quiver. After several quick blinks, I began pulling the plates down from the cabinet with the help of a kitchen chair.

The microwave beeped, notifying us that the corn had finished warming. I strained the kernels and placed a heaping tablespoon or so onto each plate. Lucinda added the sandwiches. The adults got two while children received one. Except for me. I got a tablespoon of corn, five ripped and buttered slices of bread, and a piece of American cheese.

Lucinda poured two-percent milk into small glasses, and then everyone sat.

"Thank you, girls. It looks good." Sally winked at me. She said in a loud conspirator's whisper, "The first time Lucinda learned to butter on her own, she had to eat eight pieces."

My mouth dropped open, and I looked at my new friend. She, however, avoided eye contact and studied the food on her plate.

When everyone picked up their sandwiches, I picked up two buttered pieces of bread and put the slice of cheese in between. I hoped that would make it more bearable. Then I took a bite.

I wasn't a fan of bread or butter unless cooked, and the two together were just plain gross. I slowly chewed, willing myself to swallow it. The butter warmed in my mouth and coated my teeth in an oily residue, and the bread became a wad of chewy dough on my tongue. Without meaning to, I gagged.

Sally studied me with narrowed eyes from across the table. Her lips were compressed into a white line. My heart began to trip. I took another bite and tried to hurry and swallow it, but it seemed to get caught in my throat. I quickly grabbed my milk and took a few swallows to wash it down.

By the time my first two pieces had been consumed, I was full. My glass of milk was nearly gone. Under Sally's perusal, I picked up two more pieces of bread. I made a butter sandwich out of it.

"May I get some water, please?" I asked after I'd drained the remaining milk.

"You have to eat three more pieces of bread, young lady. If you have water available, you'll get too full. I won't tolerate you wasting your food."

"Yes, ma'am," I managed.

Somehow, I choked down the rest of my meal. I drank water to wash the disgusting dough-y remains down, but I knew as soon as I stood, the food wouldn't remain for long in my stomach. In the corner of my eye, I noticed a smug smile on Sally's face.

Within five minutes, I was looking for a place to expel.

"Go outside, but stay back from the dock," Sally said. "Nick still hasn't managed to kill that gator yet."

I'd have said the required, 'yes ma'am', but I was unable. I started to retch before I left the room. I ran for the door that led behind the house. Luckily, it wasn't far: it was through the mud room off the kitchen.

I barely made it out before chunks of gooey bread mixed with pieces of milky corn spewed from my mouth. When I felt the texture going through for the second time, it made me vomit harder.

When my meal had completely passed through, I began to cry. I just wanted my mama's arms and my daddy's strength. I'd do anything to be jealous of Brycen again! *Why, oh, why did I trust a stranger?*

"Feeling sorry for yourself?" Sally asked with a knowing smile. "Grab a bucket of water and throw it onto the mess you made. Then come back inside."

Inside, Sally sat down to watch television. Once I'd reappeared, she made a point to mute the T.V. and say to Nick, "Take the airboat to the nearest store. We're nearly out of thawed bread. We'll need more for morning toast."

I could feel the blood draining out of my face. Nick grinned widely in my direction.

"Sure thing," he said with a wink at me. "Need anything else while I'm there?"

"You could get more milk and whatever kind of meat you want for breakfast."

"Okay. I'll put the gator hunt on the agenda after we eat in the morning," Nick said.

"You might pick up some flour, corn meal, more eggs, and some cooking oil as well," Sally suggested with a smile.

"You're wanting some Gator Bites, aren't you?" Nick laughed.

My mouth dropped open. *Gator Bites?* I thought. *Ewwww!*

Sally turned to me and said, "How are you feeling?"

"Fine, ma'am."

"Are you tired?"

"Yes, ma-am."

"Good," Sally said with a satisfied nod. "We're off to a good start. Until your body gets used to the chores, for about a week or so, you'll have time to yourself to rest in your room. But only for about an hour."

"Yes, ma'am."

"Use the restroom. Then go to your room."

I did just that.

Within fifteen minutes, I was locked in my little room, curled up on my mattress. Although I was very tired, I couldn't sleep. My family stared at me every time I closed my eyes. I could see Mama's love, Brycen's devotion, and Daddy's sorrow. I felt like it was all my fault that my family wasn't together. *Why hadn't I listened to Daddy?* I knew better than to talk to strangers, but the allure of Orlana on that magical afternoon had seemed too great to ignore.

When the tears began, I couldn't stop them. I cried, and I cried, and I cried. I silently sobbed until there were no more tears. I used the toilet paper to wipe my nose until it was raw. When my misery was spent, I couldn't sleep from all the swelling in my sinuses. Eventually, however, I did manage a shallow doze.

It seemed only minutes later, Sally banged the door open and loudly told me to get up.   I lurched to my feet. My body felt full of lead, and my ears seemed to buzz.

"You didn't sleep much, did you?" Sally asked. I could feel her eyes tracing my swollen features.

"No, ma'am."

"Well, I thought I worked you hard enough, but I must not have."

"Oh, no, you did!" I exclaimed in surprise.

"You'd have fallen asleep right away if I had," Sally rebutted.

"Lucinda!" she called. "Lucinda!"

"Yes, ma'am?" She appeared with a tiny curtsy.

"Teach Zoey here to deep clean the bathroom," Sally instructed. "When you're finished, get cleaned up and start supper. Make spaghetti. That should be fairly simple to cook. We'll start with fairly simple meals this week. Next week, we'll move on to a little more complex."

Lucinda nodded and grabbed me. She gently steered me toward the bathroom.

Alligator

The bathroom was small, but we worked for hours in it. We scrubbed the floors with a scrub brush, we wiped down the baseboards and walls, we scraped the lime out of the shower, and we washed and rehung the curtain. Next, we made the sink, mirror, and counter sparkle. Last, we did all the laundry for the room: we dried, folded, and put up all the towels, washcloths, and miscellaneous items. I was dragging by the end.

"Come on, girl. We still have a ways to go," Lucinda said. "I think Sally'll let you go to bed after dinner. She just had to make a point."

I only had enough energy to nod.

"Tonight, we'll just brown and crumble the hamburger for the spaghetti. Next time, I'll teach you how to make killer meatballs."

I agreed, just as I always seemed to do.

"Lucinda?" I asked quietly.

"Yes?"

"What would they've done to me if I hadn't eaten that bread?" I asked.

"I'm really glad you ate it," she whispered back. "They would've broken your spirit."

"How?"

"They would have only given you that bread to eat until you ate it. It wouldn't matter if you ate it right away or in a week. They'd have kept offering you those same slices of bread until you were so hungry you'd eat it."

I swallowed slowly, working my saliva past the huge knot in my throat.

"You, um, sound like you know... from experience."

"My spirit took some time to break, but break it they did," Lucinda confirmed. "I wish I'd just eaten it the first offering like you did. Yeah, I'd have gotten sick, too, but at least it would have been over."

I nodded grimly.

"Are we eating bread tonight?" I asked fearfully.

"I'm sure they'll want French bread with spaghetti," she said with a nod. "But it's easier to put butter on. The loaf is cut thicker and is hardier. Besides, you've had more practice now. Sally will want you to brown the burger and watch the noodles as well. After you butter the bread, we'll spread a little cheese on them and pop them in the oven. Never, I mean, never forget to set your alarm. You do *not* want to burn food around here."

"Let me guess, that's your dinner until you eat it all," I guessed.

"Bingo."

Dinner went relatively well. I didn't mess up anything big. Sally even gave me a curt nod which was a huge compliment. Nick sat down and ate two plates. Where he fit it all, I'll never know.

The other kids sat down and ate hungrily once the signal was given that it was okay. They had manners, I could tell that, but they were hungry. I was so tired that I tried to wonder what had kept them busy all day, but I found I just couldn't pay attention enough to care.

After the meal was over, we had to clean the kitchen. Then, finally, I was sent to the bathroom (which I admired as I prepared myself for bed). When I went to my room, I was locked in. I was glad to escape from work. I was so exhausted, I sank on my bed and immediately fell into a deep sleep. Thankfully, I didn't even dream.

I slept the entire night through. When Sally opened the door and instructed me to get up, I looked around blurry-eyed, trying to remember where I was. When I did, all the mourning for my family hit me anew.

I staggered to my feet, feeling as if my heart had been shredded. I took a steadying breath and slipped on my shoes. I followed Sally out of my room. I headed to the restroom while she continued toward the kitchen. As soon as I shuffled in, Sally barked out an order.

"Make French Toast today," she said.

When the big woman left the room to wake the others, Lucinda said, "Don't worry. You won't rip the bread with this meal. We soak the slices in a mixture of eggs, milk, vanilla, cinnamon, and a little sugar, and then we cook them. The biggest thing to watch is to make sure they don't burn. It's actually a simple meal to prepare."

I nodded and smiled at Lucinda. I was still fighting my boiling emotions.

"Hey, kid, it's okay," she said with empathy.

It made my lips tremble. To prevent the flood of emotions, Lucinda gave me a chore to help take my mind off my misery.

The meal went well enough. Everyone seemed to enjoy the breakfast, and nothing criticizing was said. Jez, Javier, and Deidra all tried to send me a wordless thank you with a quick look, but nothing more; they were watched like hawks.

Mealtimes were very quiet instances. The only talking that was done was basically by Sally and Nick. The solitary moments someone else spoke was in direct response to something one of them had asked. Not even Lucinda was allowed conversation.

It was obvious that Lucinda and I were considered the food people. Not only did we prepare the meals and clean up afterwards, but we were expected to wait on and serve those at the table as well.

In between our food preparations, we were given other cleaning chores. There was no down time except for maybe fifteen minutes mid-morning and mid-afternoon. Other than that, we worked. I was very surprised I didn't run into the other children. They were so busy doing other chores with either Sally or Nick, I rarely caught a glimpse.

This morning was one I'll never forget. As soon as Nick had eaten his fill of the cuisine, he took the hunk of fish from the refrigerator to the sink.

He tossed a few words over his shoulder at us, "Give me a minute before you start to clean, girls."

Then he left for a short time and came back. He held a huge hook anchored to a braided rope. After baiting the hook, he loaded his rifle and went out the door leading to the mud room.

Right when we finished up the kitchen, there was a loud rifle shot. I jumped with a start.

"It's okay, Zoey," Lucinda soothed. "We're gonna have Gator Bites for supper, I'll bet."

"Ewww," I said softly.

"Don't let them hear you say that," Lucinda warned. "If they ever hear you complain about anything, that is what you'll get to eat for a month. Every meal. And there are plenty of Gators to go around."

My shoulders drooped. "Thanks for letting me know," I whispered sincerely.

"I'm just warning you to help," Lucinda said. "I don't want you learning the hard way... like I did."

"I appreciate it," I responded. *What else could I say to that?*

Within the hour, Nick came in and laid a giant hunk of pinkish-white meat in the sink. Without a word, he turned and went back outside.

"Where's he going?" I asked.

"He's going back to process the rest of the alligator," Lucinda said. "He'll remove the skin and cure it to sell. He'll also get any more good meat off. When he brings it in, we'll have to cut and package it. We'll leave enough out to cook for lunch."

Lucinda and I began to cut the tail up into chunks. Most pieces were in one-inch diameters. We saved enough for lunch. Lucinda showed me how to wrap the rest with freezer paper and add a date. Then we put them in the freezer.

"Alligator reminds me of pork. The meat looks a lot like it," Lucinda said.

"Really?"

"Yes. It kind of tastes like pork... or chicken."

"Doesn't everything taste like chicken?" I asked.

Lucinda giggled then covered her mouth.

"What's wrong?" I asked.

"Never let Sally, or Nick for that matter, hear you laugh. You're not allowed to have fun," Lucinda informed.

"Really?" I asked.

"Really. I'd never see you again if they knew we enjoyed each other."

I swallowed slowly then mixed up the eggs and milk together while Lucinda showed me how to proportion the flour to corn meal with seasoning. When the batter was prepared, we put the hunks of meat in it and began frying.

"Gator is easier to cook than chicken," Lucinda informed. "Probably because it's cut into smaller pieces."

I nodded.

From the doorway, Sally's voice commanded us. "Lucinda, you let Zoey cook now. You've shown her, and the faster we get her trained, the sooner I get paid."

"Yes, ma'am," Lucinda said.

"I think Zoey has gotten the hang of buttering bread, so you prepare the garlic bread and let her learn something new."

"Yes, ma'am," Lucinda replied again.

Lucinda handed me the metal mesh spoon to retrieve the Gator Bites when they finished cooking. I slowly turned them in the oil. When they were a nice golden-brown, I placed them in a bowl full of paper towels and added a quick dash of salt. Sally watched us like hawks.

"Zoey, set the table. You need to learn to multitask."

I gave the gator one last stir, removed a few pieces that were ready, then grabbed the plates. It was the last batch to cook, so it was nearly meal time. Lucinda was preparing green beans.

I laid out plates, utensils, and cups. Then I dashed back to check the meat. Sally was still watching.

The pieces were a little darker than the rest. They were a bronze color and were beginning to smoke. In a rush of nervousness, I scooped them up then accidentally dropped the wire ladle. The food splattered across the floor.

"Pick it up. Nooooow!" Sally barked angrily.

I went to grab a hot pad, but Sally said, "NO, ma'am! You'll use your hands!"

I tried to pick it up, but it was so hot, I dropped it automatically.

"Get a plate and put the pieces on it. You will use your hands," Sally said slowly. She deliberately enunciated each syllable.

I grabbed a plate and then quickly picked up the pieces and put them on the plate.

"Set that plate at your spot," Sally said.

I had no other choice, so I did as I was told. A blister was already forming on my hand from touching the piece of sizzling gator.

Sally was now behind me. She grabbed my wrist and then pressed my hand down on top of my meat. I cried out in pain.

Luckily, the fried bites had cooled just a little, but it was still very hot.

"Next time, you'll remember to check the meat faster. Even if it means you have to come back to setting the table. Now get up and help Lucinda fill the rest of the plates and cups."

I asked, "Ma'am, may I please wash my hands? They're greasy, and I don't want to drop the milk." I blinked back tears.

"I don't want you to be a klutz, so yes, please."

After everyone was served, I sat down to eat. I knew my eyes were still shimmering with tears. I quickly brushed them away. Lucinda's warning echoed in my ears, so I knew I had to eat the reptile tail on my plate.

The first bite actually didn't taste that bad. Just the thought of chewing the killed animal's tail that had been picked up off the floor made a huge ball in my throat that was hard to swallow around.

Sally watched me closely. She nodded ever so slightly when she saw me swallow and put another piece in my mouth.

After the meal, washing the dishes was rough. My hands hurt where they were burned, but I somehow made it without any more reprimands. Lucinda kept giving me sympathetic looks. I could tell she wanted

to console me but dared not while the drill sergeant
was within ear shot.

Deidra's Departure

It was early when Sally barged into my room. She flipped on the harsh light and said, "Get up. We need to go on an outing."

I just blinked several times before her words sunk in.

Sally turned and began waddling away when she called back over her shoulder, "Make oatmeal and toast for breakfast."

"Yes, ma'am," I replied.

I scrambled to my feet and shuffled to the restroom. I quickly got ready and met Lucinda in the kitchen.

"I can't help you this morning," Lucinda whispered to me. "I have to help get the others ready."

"What's going on?" I asked back. There was an urgency in her voice, and her stress was infectious.

"Deidra is meeting her new family. You all have to go as part of your training. Be on your best behavior today," Lucinda warned. "Consequences if you don't are... well, you don't want to find out."

I looked up at her. I could feel my eyes widen with fear. I nodded emphatically, and took out pans to start boiling water. While I was waiting on the water to boil, I toasted and buttered the bread. My fingers still throbbed from the blisters, but I did my best to ignore the discomfort.

I set the table and had the oatmeal ready in hot, steaming bowls. Lightly buttered toast waited on sparkling white plates. I filled freshly squeezed orange juice into the clear glasses. Two cups of coffee waited patiently on the adults. Then I hovered by the table nervously.

Finally, in what seemed like hours later, the others shuffled in. Lucinda, Jez, Javier, and Deidra were all in somber moods while Sally was very animated and happy. There was no change in Nick's behavior. He sauntered in with his normal swagger.

The children all sat down and placed a paper towel on their laps. Mechanically, they reached for their spoons to scoop creamy oatmeal into their mouths.

"You're finally accomplished at making an oatmeal and toast breakfast," Sally said with a glance my way.

"Thank you, ma'am," I replied quickly. The others' mood of scared obedience was rubbing off on me. Suddenly, I wasn't hungry.

"You may sit and eat," Sally permitted.

"Yes, ma'am," I responded. I sat but didn't pick up my spoon.

Nick glanced at me and then back down at his plate. He hungrily wolfed down his meal. Lucinda caught my eye and nodded ever so slightly toward my plate, so I took a bite of my toast.

A short while after the kitchen was cleaned up, everyone piled into the older model Suburban. No one said a word for at least thirty minutes.

"Drive to the Super Hotel by the mall. We'll meet in the parking lot," Sally told Nick.

He grunted a reply.

Sally turned around to look at the four of us in the back. "I don't need to tell you to be on your best behavior. You're not to speak unless spoken to. If you're asked a question, look at me before you respond. If I nod, you may answer. If I do not, then you best keep your mouth shut. Do I make myself clear?"

Five voices uttered, "Yes, ma'am."

When Sally turned back around, I shuddered. *Was this what it would be like when I met my new family?* I shook my head slightly. That wasn't the right term for the new people we would soon be living with. Family meant loving arms and acceptance. People who bought children to be slaves were not family.

Another twenty minutes stretched by. Still, no one said a word. We all would touch Deidra from time to time to show our support. The fear radiating off her was palpable, and I noticed a tear shining in the corner of her eye.

My heart went out to her. I wanted to comfort her, but *how could I?* I had no idea of the kind of people we were meeting. I think the fear of the unknown was more terrible than facing what we were living with presently, but really, *how much worse could it be?*

When we pulled up in the enormous parking lot, we chose a secluded place near the back. The palm trees sheltered the car with large fronds. They reminded me of green umbrellas extending over us.

Nick shut the suburban off, and we all got out to stretch our legs. I breathed in the humid late morning air.   I smelled the fragrance of near-by flowers, and a few birds chirped from the tree to my left.   It was the most I'd enjoyed being outside in the past few months.

A cobalt blue Audi pulled up.   The sports car was so quiet it purred.   A couple dressed in expensive-looking clothing got out.   The man offered a quick smile and a firm handshake.   The woman also smiled but didn't offer her hand to Sally or Nick.

"Ah, Deidra," the man said.   "You look just like the pictures and video.   You'll fit in perfectly with our family."   He flashed a warm smile at her.

Deidra looked petrified.

"It's okay, honey," the woman said softly.   "You'll do well.   You're going to be a big sister to a three-year-old girl and a toddler boy.   Your job is going to be looking after them."

Sally said, "She's been trained on cooking and cleaning, but we didn't have toddlers to train her with," she paused.   "However, she has the disposition and is highly trainable.   If you're unhappy with her service for any reason, you may send her back to me for an update with discipline."

Sally pushed Deidra toward the couple.   The dark-haired girl took a few awkward steps and looked back at me and Lucinda.   It was like watching a panicked animal roll its eyes in fear.

The woman soothed, "It's okay. You'll enjoy your new home, honey."

The man asked Sally, "You received the transaction, I assume?"

"Yes, I did. Thank you very much," she replied.

"You come highly recommended. Thanks again," the man shook her hand in departure.

"We'll be in touch," Sally called to them as they were loading Deidra in their vehicle.

With a curt nod, they slowly backed out of their spot and were gone. Sally watched until they were out of sight.

"Well, as a small step in your training and to celebrate, we're going to go eat some custard as a treat. I'm in a giving mood," Sally said with a smile.

We all piled back into the suburban. Deidra's spot looked startlingly empty. *Celebrate? How could we celebrate?* I felt empty and sad.

"Hey," Lucinda breathed in my ear. "She's going to a good home. I've seen enough to get a feel. She's in a better place than we are."

I nodded past the lump in my throat. My stomach rumbled from lack of food, but I was fairly certain I was not going to be able to "celebrate".

A short while later, we parked at the famous Alaya's Frozen Custard. Nick shut the vehicle off. All our eyes wandered to Sally.

"You all may get out and come to the window with me. You may order vanilla or chocolate custard with one topping of your choice. We'll eat and then go back to do our chores. Best behavior!" she reminded us merrily with a wink.

Vaguely, I wondered exactly how much money she got for Deidra. It must be a lot. I really didn't know what was considered a lot of money, but I know it made Sally happy and in a generous enough mood to buy us ice cream whether we wanted it or not.

Where Sally's mood was bubbly, ours was somber, but that seemed to just make her happier. As we spooned the soothing coolness into our mouths, she chatted happily with Nick. All too soon, we were loaded back in the suburban and headed in the direction of the bleak swampiness offered by our training home.

The Underlying Threat

Originally, I think Sally was only going to keep me for six months or so before I was to live with the new family. However, she ended up keeping me for nearly an entire year. The people wanted my training in the kitchen to be more extensive. They expected the nearly nine-year-old girl they were to receive to be a chef's rival.

On top of being an expert cook, I had to be very knowledgeable about deep cleaning. Oftentimes, I found myself tearing up at the level of expectation pressing down on me, suffocating me. Other times, I threw myself into my work to keep from thinking.

Lucinda and I were the only two in the house now. Two months or so after Deidra left, Jez and Javier also were placed. Their leaving was traumatic to me, but not nearly as bad as Deidra's. I know it was because I knew more of what to expect, and I wasn't quite as close with them. No matter how I looked at it, I was next, and it scared me.

Lucinda was always there. She grew to be like a sister to me. In fact, because she was the only one who really cared about me in this new existence, I knew I'd always think of her as one.

"Lucinda, I just can't scrub anymore," I complained. "My arms are killing me!"

I was on my hands and knees with a brush, literally scrubbing the thick laminate. I'd been at it for hours. My knees were bruised from the constant pressure against the relentless surface.

Lucinda sponged up the excess water in my wake and checked my work. Additionally, she wiped down the baseboards with every inch of progress. If I missed any spot, I had to go back and redo it. Lucinda was my friend, but she also saved me from worse punishment if our jailer deemed my work as mediocre.

"You have to, Zoey. If you don't, you'll have *Sally* to contend with." Some of Lucinda's animosity was evident in the lowered whisper.

"Can't we take a break?" I whined. "My arms are going to fall off."

"You can go ask *Sally* if we can," she responded slyly. Her eyes narrowed when she uttered the name, "If she doesn't agree, then just look at it as making your muscles stronger."

I threw Lucinda a mild glare. There truly wasn't any hostility directed at her, but I wanted her to know my level of irritation.

I grumbled delicately under my breath as I pushed the brush onto the surface for what seemed like the millionth time. I bit back a groan as I moved my hands in circular patterns. My muscles were screaming at me. Ribbons of agony rifled up and down my shoulders and across my back with each push. My arms truly did feel that they could just detach and fall down onto the sparkling wood theme at any time.

We'd been at this for two days. Not only did we scrub the floor and wipe the baseboards, but we also washed the walls, dusted, and cleaned the windows. Then, Lucinda would unscrew the light fixtures and hand them to me to wash with soapy water and dry. She would remove any dust that remained and then replace the sparkling light fixtures. Lastly, we'd oil the baseboards and wood trim around the windows. It was exhausting.

We'd already cleaned each of the bedrooms, the hall, the bathroom, and now we were finally on the kitchen. After we made lunch, we'd start in the mudroom.   However, my thoughts scattered as Sally entered with an armload of groceries.

She instructed, "After you finish the kitchen, take a thirty-minute break. You'll do the mud room tomorrow. I want you to make a pot pie from scratch this evening."

"Yes, ma-am," I responded as cheerily as I could through my gritted teeth. When I received a stern look from Sally, I offered a shaky, apologetic smile.

"That was borderline, young lady. If I hear any other disrespect in your tone, you will cook but not eat. Do you understand me?"

"Yes, ma'am," I said miserably. I bent my head with cowed submission.

"Good."

Sally turned on her heel and went to the living room. I heard the crunch of the fabric as it settled under our dictator's considerable weight. Shortly after, the television flicked on.

We finished the kitchen, and I was drooping. Lucinda looked at me kindly.

"Go lay down, Zoey," she said with a gentle push toward my room. "You know how much work pot pies are. I can help you by cutting up some of the vegetables while you take a quick nap. Don't worry, I'll wake you up on time."

"She probably won't let you help me because it's *part of my training*," I sneered. I wrinkled my nose to emphasize my feelings.

Lucinda couldn't help herself. She giggled quietly at my animations.

"Besides," I added. "Aren't you tired, too?"

"Yes," Lucinda admitted, "but you had the hardest work. I don't mind."

"Just wait," I requested. "We can do it together."

Forty minutes later, we were chopping vegetables. I sliced celery and gave the onions to Lucinda after I'd played on her sympathies. I snickered when the pungent smell became more distinctive, and I saw her eyes water up. I cleared my throat to cover the sound of us having fun.

We both cut up carrots and diced potatoes. I prepared the chicken while Lucinda sautéed the vegetables together. I baked the bottom pie crusts a little before tossing the ingredients with some thyme and seasoning and then sealing them between crusts.

Before long, I pulled two lightly golden pies out of the hot oven. They billowed clouds of aromatic steam. One could almost taste the thick fillings of creamy gravy, diced vegetables, and shredded chicken.

Nick's eyes gleamed as I placed a large wedge onto a plate. Lucinda laid it before him. He was like a toddler with cake on his birthday. Immediately, he grabbed up a fork and prepared to shovel it into his mouth.

"Don't you dare take a bite, Nick," growled Sally. "We will eat in a civilized manner and wait for everyone to be seated."

"Those two?" he indicated with a slight nod in their direction.

"They're all we have left here, so yes. They'll pour our glasses after setting the food in the appropriate spots. When they've seated themselves, we'll eat."

"It seems strange that we don't have other trainees yet," Nick grunted.

"We're going hunting tomorrow."

All heads swiveled to look at Sally. I froze in surprise. No new recruits had been brought in since my presence. I felt my mouth gape open.

"We have a nice nest egg, but funds are starting to ebb away. We need to start on a new stockpile," Sally said simply.

"You trust them two here together?" Nick wagged a finger toward us.

"Yes. Lucinda knows what will happen, but you're right. Perhaps Zoey has forgotten."

I could feel my eyes and ears prick up. *Lucinda and I were going to be alone here? Tomorrow*? I swallowed.

"Don't forget I know you have a brother," Sally said suggestively. Her brown eyes bored into mine.

"Wh – what?" I stuttered. I gripped the back of the nearest chair.

Sally said sternly, "Don't get any wise ideas. I can trick your brother, just like I tricked you, if you try a disappearing act."

"Wh – what?" I repeated. I slowly sunk to the cold, hard chair.

"I think you hit a nerve," Nick snickered uncaringly. "It doesn't appear to be sinking in."

"It means if you try to run, your brother is going to be here in your place. I won't be very forgiving, either. I'll be *especially* hard on him. Then, I *will* find you. You'll either be here, locked up in solitary confinement, or you'll be alligator meat, so you won't get to help him adjust."

"That's true," Nick agreed. "You go wandering and step off in the wrong spot, those gators will see what a sweet treat they can make of you."

"I – I won't... run!" I strangled out. My heart was beating super hard and sweat popped out over my body. My breath was caught in my chest.

"You're giving her a panic attack, Sally," Nick observed.

"Force yourself to slow down your breathing," Sally commanded. Then, in a slightly softer voice, she added, "If you promise to stay here and not try anything foolish, I won't target your brother."

"I – I," I struggled to get out. I gasped. No more words would come.

Lucinda got up and stood behind me. She put her hands on my shoulders and squeezed them slightly. She bent over and talked softly in my ear. She was careful to speak loud enough for the others to hear.

"Zoey, take a long, slow breath."

As soon as I complied, she gave me another command. "Now, what is three plus five?"

"Eight," I gasped. I squeezed my eyes closed, and a tear leaked out.

"Three times ten?"

"Th - thirty."

"Eight times Eight?"

"Sixty-four." I opened my eyes into the kind face of my soul sister.

The fist squeezing my heart was starting to let up just a bit. My breath was more regular, and my muscles were finally beginning to loosen. Silence filled the room for a short span, probably to help facilitate my recovery. Finally, Sally's harsh voice shattered the simulated stillness.

"You've been working with her on math?" she coldly asked Lucinda.

"Um, y – yes, ma'am." My acting sister looked up suddenly. Her eyes were enormous.

Sally gave us a hard stare, and I hiccuped. The catch in my throat threatened to close again.

The large woman let out a long, slow breath. It was obvious that she was trying to calm herself.

"That's good, Lucinda. She needs to have some math skills with cooking and such. Next time, however? *Run it by me first*." Those hard, mean eyes narrowed dangerously.

"Yes, ma'am." Lucinda gave a quick curtsy.

"Now, Zoey?" Sally asked. Her unforgiving stare focused on me once again.

"Ma'am?" I squeaked out.

"Do I have your word, you will behave yourself and stay put in this house with Lucinda?"

"Yes, ma'am."

"Good."

"Does... does that m – mean you won't..." my voice trailed off.

"No, I won't target your brother if you're a good girl," Sally agreed with a decisive nod. "Now eat your dinner and clean up the kitchen. You may rest afterward. I know you've been working hard lately." Surprisingly, her tone had softened.

"Yes, ma'am," I managed. "Thank you."

I picked up my fork and stared at my plate. Finally, I put a small bite in my mouth, but it was some time before I was able to manufacture enough saliva to swallow the soft food. Sally watched me like a hawk, but she didn't issue any more commands. When they were finished eating, she and Nick vacated the room.

A Day Alone

Early the next morning, Lucinda awoke me.

"Get up, Zoey. We need to make a good breakfast. Let's do a spinach-bacon-mushroom quiche. We have the necessary ingredients. At least that will put our jailers in a better mood. Sally is always happy when she sees you master another dish."

"Okay," I said sleepily and sat up.

While I prepared the pie crust, Lucinda took out a big bag of oranges. She busied herself slicing the fruit as I pressed the dough into the pan.

"What are we going to do today?" I whispered. "We've cleaned the whole house from top to bottom."

"Don't worry," Lucinda replied. "I'm sure Sally will have a list."

I sighed uneasily. I didn't trust Sally, and I was sure she didn't trust me. However, she may think my spirit was completely broken after my display last night. To be honest, I wasn't sure that it wasn't. I had no desire to put my brother at risk.

"It'd be nice if we could relax a bit," I said.

Lucinda snickered. "That'll be the day." She paused and then pressed her fingers to her lips and whispered, "but we'll find a way to have a little fun. When the cats are away, the mice will play... just a little bit anyway."

I saw my happiness reflected in her smile.

The quiche was baked to perfection. The polished surface was speckled with a few golden freckles, and the cheese baked on top was gooey in some spots and was slightly crispy in others. The pie crust was flaky and light. My mouth watered at the scent.

We cut the casserole into slices and put a generous amount on each plate. Lucinda filled glasses with freshly squeezed orange juice. I quickly added slices of lightly buttered toast.

When Sally and Nick shuffled in, they had pleasant looks of surprise on their faces.

"What's this?" Sally crooned.

Nick rubbed his stomach in anticipation. He slid into his seat and drummed his fingers lightly on the table top.

"It's a bacon-spinach-portobello quiche," I said. "It was Lucinda's idea."

"It looks delicious," Sally approved. She offered a small smile of thanks.

Nick's eyes darted back and forth from people to the casserole. I was aware of his approval without a comment.

When we were all seated, we seemed to pick up our forks in synchronicity. I nearly giggled, but then I remembered the seriousness of their outing and sobered immediately. Still, I couldn't stop the light, happy feeling in my chest. It was a day, the first one since I'd met them, that I'd be Sally-and-Nick free!

We bit into the light but calorie-heavy food. The rich custard-like texture melted in our mouths. It was creamy deliciousness.

Nick was already reaching for seconds.

"Did you even taste that?" Sally admonished. She slid him a sideways glance.

"You bet I did," Nick replied without missing a beat. "That's why I'm getting more."

Sally didn't respond, but a short while later, she also held her plate for seconds. I smiled shyly at her as I dished another generous helping onto her dinnerware.

Nick held up his coffee cup, so Lucinda capped it.

"I'm very proud of you girls for showing initiative," Sally said.

"Thank you," we both murmured.

"But no cooking while Nick and I are out. You may warm up leftovers or soup with the microwave, or you can make yourselves sandwiches. I have bologna and cheese or peanut butter and jelly."

"Yes, ma'am," we replied in unison.

"We'll be gone overnight. You. Had. Better. Not. Pull. Anything. Do you understand?"

We both sucked in fearful breaths and nodded.

"I can't hear you," she enunciated.

"Yes, ma'am," we said breathlessly.

"Don't think by buttering me up with a nice breakfast that I'm fooled. In fact, it makes me suspicious. *Are* you up to something?" Her eyes rocketed back and forth between us.

"N – no, ma'am," I said with a small curtsy.

Lucinda said, "Oh, no, ma'am. We just wanted to show off Zoey's cooking skills. We thought you'd enjoy a good breakfast before you leave."

She continued to study us before finally nodding and rising from the table.

"I have a list of chores for you to do while we're gone, but it's not a hard list. I should have saved the deep cleaning for today, but plans change." She shrugged. "Anyway, you'll have a little more down time than normal, but you deserve it."

"Yes, ma'am," I curtsied deeply to show my gratitude.

"Respect my generosity, and don't make me regret it," she added, and her eyes narrowed.

Our heads nodded a response.

Ten minutes after they'd gone, Lucinda and I did a happy dance. We giggled and laughed until we had no breath left. We swung each other around until we were dizzy. Then we fell on the floor and just enjoyed not working for a time.

"What do you say we do all the work today and just play and have a day off tomorrow?" Lucinda asked.

"*Really*?" I said.

"Really. Who knows when they'll get back. We may only get the morning off, but I want to have our work done early so they won't be in a bad mood."

"Okay," I said happily. I was *free*... for a day. I hadn't had a day off from chores and work for nearly a year. I didn't think anything could dampen my spirits.

It was about four o'clock in the afternoon when we finished everything. Sally was right, it was an easy list compared to what we were normally expected to do.

"Let's eat peanut butter and jelly then do you think we could watch a little television?" I asked.

"I don't see why not. Sally didn't say we couldn't."

"Yay! I haven't gotten to see any T.V. for a year."

Lucinda didn't say anything but nodded.

"Lucinda?" I asked.

"Yes?" She glanced at me.

"I don't mean this to sound weird, but... I love you. Thank you for helping me here."

"I feel the same, Zoe. You're my little sister. I'm really going to miss you when you leave."

It was a sobering statement. Although I'd never want to stay here, I felt strings pull down hard on my heart. Then the feeling shifted and began to balloon up inside me. It welled until the bursting point.

"I don't want to leave you, Lucinda!" I blurted.

"I don't want you to, either. But on a good note, though, you get away from *here*," she said honestly. "This is not a good place to be."

"Lucinda, why can't you leave?" I asked.

"Because they value my help too much," she replied honestly. "They don't have the patience to help kids adjust. They leave that and the great bulk of the training to me."

"But, where did *you* come from?" I pressed.

Lucinda looked down sadly. "I – I was abandoned," she said. She lowered her half-eaten sandwich to the plate.

"*What?*" I asked. I shook my head and then bound over. I wrapped my arms around her and pulled her in close. "That can't be true. I can't imagine *anyone* not wanting *you!*"

"I don't know who my father is," she countered, "and my mom was a drug addict. She was passed out on the street, basically. It happened daily. Sally and Nick came by and noticed. It was all too easy for them to pluck me up. Honestly, they saved me from a more horrible life."

"But you can't feel grateful to them!" I argued incredulously.

"I *do,* in a way, but mostly? I don't. I see what they do to others. I see how they rip people apart just to make money. They make slaves of kids. It's horrible and abusive. All I'm saying is that she saved *me* from a worse life. They know I have nowhere to go, so there's safety in trusting me in their eyes."

A pregnant pause followed her revelation. I had to let all that sink in. I was still pretty young to truly understand abandonment issues or drug use. I knew it must happen because I do recall my parents warning me away from drugs, but it was hard for me to understand the abandonment thing when my family wanted me. *Really* wanted me, so I did my best to empathize with Lucinda.

I finally asked, "Is Nick related to Sally?"

The look on Lucinda's face was deeply relieved. She took a breath and squared her shoulders.

"Thank you, Zoey, for not judging me."

"I love you like my sister, Lucinda," I said simply.

"And I love you. Thanks for changing the subject. To answer your question, Nick is Sally's younger brother."

"B – but..." my voice trailed off.

"Yes, I know. Sally is a big lady while Nick is little. I think they may've had different fathers. I'm not sure about that part, and I'm not about to ask. But it wouldn't surprise me."

I nodded in agreement.

"Are you okay to finish your sandwich?" I tentatively asked.

She nodded and picked it up.

Within a half hour, we were perched on the couch with the television on. We found old television shows. We watched Bewitched, Gilligan's Island, and I Dream of Jeannie. We watched an old western called Bonanza. We didn't move from there all night.

The next morning, we warmed up the quiche. It was fairly good leftover, but not quite as creamy, and the crust was a little soggy. Still, it was better than a sandwich.

"What do you want to do today?" I asked.

"You know, I'd like to play cards. I know where a deck is. Wanna play a few games?"

"Really?" I asked. I know my expression had to reflect what I was feeling inside: adventurous unease. I wanted desperately to play, actually *play a game*, but fear held me back.

Finally, I stuttered, "B – but *should* we?"

"It's okay, Zoey," Lucinda soothed. "I know where Nick keeps a deck. I wouldn't touch one of Sally's, but he's not as careful as she is. I'll put it back exactly how I found it, okay? We can hear them coming a long time before they get here, so let's have some fun."

I finally felt like a tiny window had opened. I allowed myself a moment, just a snatch of time, to feel like a girl of nearly nine. *It was permissible for a nine-year-old to want to play a game.*

"Okay," I said and held my breath.

Lucinda bounced up and ran for Nick's area by his recliner. She snatched the cards as if the bookshelf would burn her and returned.

"What do you want to play?" she asked.

"Go Fish?"

"You bet!" Lucinda smiled.

For the next couple of hours, we simply played games. In addition to Go Fish, we played War, Crazy Eights, and Rummy. Then we watched more television. It seemed like a lifetime ago, maybe someone else's lifetime, where I had so indulged. It would make it all the more difficult when *they* returned.

They still weren't back by lunch. I looked through the pantry even though I was sure I'd memorized all the items in there.

"Didn't she say we could make soup?" I asked.

"Yes, but are you sure you want soup?   It's already hot."   She wiped a hand across her forehead for effect.

"Kinda.   She'll probably make us eat bologna for supper, and I really don't want that or PB and J right now."

"Fine.   What kind?" Lucinda asked.

"Bean with Bacon?"

"You bet!" she nodded.

"Do you think I should just warm it up in the microwave, or do you think it'd be okay to use the stove top?" I asked.

"Better use the microwave.   I don't want her to catch us 'cooking'."
"Okay."

Newbies

It was nearly dark when the car finally pulled down the enormously long drive. I was on pins and needles because I didn't know what to expect. I paced the room.

"Just act as normal as you can," Lucinda advised. "Stay out of the way and above all, don't react. The new kids will be scared. Do *not* interfere."

"Okay," I answered a little breathlessly.

"Come on," Lucinda instructed. "Let's go in the kitchen so we're even *more* out of the way. I have no idea what kind of mood they'll be in."

I meekly followed my friend into the kitchen. I heard the crunch of the gravel and the car shut off. For some reason, my heart began beating harder.

Sally opened the door for Nick. He shuffled in carrying two children, one on each hip. Their backs were to me.

"Put them in the same room for tonight. Put them in Zoey's room, the one without a window. She can move into Jez's old room. Zoey won't be with us much longer, anyway."

I felt the jack hammer begin pounding on my rib cage. *I wouldn't be with them much longer?* I didn't know how to feel about that.

I heard the noises of Sally preparing the kids in the room. They began crying immediately. They couldn't have been older than six.

"Does she normally bring back children that young?" I whispered to Lucinda.

"Typically, she brings back between seven and eight-year-olds because they're big enough to work and can learn harder stuff, but sometimes she gets younger children and sells them to clients who can't have kids. Those two are in-betweeners. They could be either or."

"I hope they go to some family together." My heart was sick at the thought of them being split up. They'd already lost their parents.

"Me, too. It'll be rough around here if they don't," Lucinda agreed.

"How do we act? I don't know what to do," I admitted. I realized I was wringing my hands.

"The best thing for now is to stay right here until we're instructed otherwise."

I took in a deep, slow breath. "Okay."

I think about an hour passed before we saw either Sally or Nick. They both came into the kitchen and sat heavily at the table. Crying with intermittent screams reverberated down the hall.

Sally said, "Please fix five grilled cheese sandwiches and additional ones if you're hungry."

"Yes, ma'am," I said. Lucinda and I turned toward the fridge to retrieve the necessary materials.

"Zoey, you're to sleep in Jez's old room. The other one is now occupied."

"Yes, ma'am," I repeated.

"Starting tomorrow, Lucinda, you're to spend each day with the twins. Zoey, you'll be on your own in the kitchen, now. You'll prepare everything by yourself. It's the final step to sending you on your merry way."

I had no choice in the matter, so I curtsied and began buttering the bread slices. I could feel Sally's eyes pressing against my back, but she didn't say anything more to me.

I blinked back tears as I mechanically put the pan on the stove top and turned the heat to low-medium. As much as I wanted to be free from this... place, I couldn't imagine losing Lucinda. She was all I had left.

"They're twins?" I heard Lucinda ask. She was removing the cheese from the plastic. She placed each slice on a plate for my use when I was ready.

"Yes. One girl and one boy. I got lucky. I have a family who wants a girl and a boy. What a lucky find that I managed to get just what they wanted with one outing," Sally said.

"But, won't that make them easier to spot?" Lucinda asked.

I realized that Lucinda meant the police might be looking for the children.

"Not where they're going," Sally replied.

I could hear the smile in her voice. I flipped the current sandwich I was cooking and set out a plate.

"What is it that you want me to teach them, ma'am?" Lucinda inquired. "I assume they won't be made to work."

"Teach them manners and compliance, mostly," Sally instructed. "Teach them to clean up after themselves, to brush their teeth. You know, that kind of thing.”

I turned and placed a plate in front of Sally. I added a glass of cold milk to accompany it.

“Will Nick be in soon? If so, I’ll prepare his plate next,” I offered.

Sally nodded. “That will be fine. He should be in shortly.”

That evening, I went to the new room. The decor was just as void of emotion as my last spot. A cold twin-sized bed waited in the corner next to a bare, flea market-worthy chest of drawers. The best thing about the place was that there was a window that let in some natural light. I snorted. *Not that I’d be in the room while light was available.*

I set my alarm and crawled into the sheets. The springs creaked under me. It was odd to hear that sound again because I’d been sleeping on a mattress on the floor for nearly a year now.

I had difficulty when I tried to fall asleep. Every time I closed my eyes, I saw Deidra’s face on that long car ride to meet her family. I also saw the other two kids when they met the new people who would control their lives. Javier’s home was as sad as this place, but I felt that Jez’s home would be much better.

I imagined Lucinda’s face pressed against the living room window, watching me leave when it was my turn. Worst of all, I remembered Mama, Daddy, and Brycen and pictured their pain when they couldn’t find me on my eighth birthday.

The next morning, I was weary when the alarm blared, but I was even more tired of trying to sleep, so it was almost a welcoming sound. I dragged myself out of bed.

I quickly decided to make pancakes. It was simple and quick, and what kid didn't like pancakes? I wanted to make something the newbies might like since they had to be experiencing trauma. I hoped Sally was easier on the younger kids than she was on me. There was solace in my heart when I remembered Lucinda would be working closely with them and not Sally.

There was a warm pile of lightly golden pancakes stacked on a dish in the center of the table when the others entered the kitchen. Plates and utensils were gleaming at each spot, and I had milk and orange juice pitchers ready to pour into the glasses. I'd heated up maple syrup and had softened butter for any who wanted it.

Sally and Nick sat and automatically picked up their steaming mugs of coffee to sip. They seemed to be in decent moods. Lucinda appeared in the doorway with two small shapes in front of her. Gently, she herded them toward the table.

The girl had coppery brown waves that spilled down her back, and darkly fringed eyes. Her brother had a slightly richer shade of hair, but his eyes were a startling blue. Currently, both were staring at the table. When they saw Sally, their lips puckered fearfully.

"Aw, now, don't do that," Sally admonished. "I won't hurt you." She leaned back, in a relaxed manner, trying to demonstrate that she wasn't going to approach them.

"I want my mommy!" the little girl cried. She huddled into Lucinda until only one eye peeked at the large woman.

The boy's brows crinkled down and his lips were pursed in a sulky pout. He didn't move.

"I know you do, but you have to get used to life without them," Sally said unsympathetically. "If you want to eat, you'll need to sit quietly. If you want to cry, you'll need to return to your room without eating."

The children stood, frozen, reminding me of petrified animals unsure of where to turn. Lucinda squatted down and talked softly to them, encouraging them to eat. She straightened and softly ruffled their hair.

I moved to the two chairs farthest from Sally and Nick. "Here," I said, pulling out the furniture and patting the seats invitingly. "I made pancakes for you."

I was still bent over. I tried to make myself less threatening to them by stooping to their level. I did my best to encourage them to eat.

I smiled and asked softly, "Do you like pancakes?"

When Lucinda tried to guide them to their seats, both children dug their heels in and began to scream.

Sally stood abruptly and barked, "Take them back to their rooms!"

Lucinda quickly retreated with the twins. My heart shattered into a million pieces. I could hear the silent shards tinkling on the floor, but I did my best to mask my emotions. I still was required to wait on the sergeants and clean up the mess.

After the adults left the kitchen, I put the remaining pancakes in the fridge. I didn't eat nor did Lucinda. I knew better than to waste food. I was sure that we'd revisit the items at lunch.

The next few weeks went about the same. On occasion, the children sat and ate with us, but more often than not, they were sent to their rooms to throw fits of terror. As a punishment, they went without eating.

After several weeks of this, the children's resolve weakened. Lucinda became their family, and I was the other safe person. They were sullen and withdrawn around Sally and Nick. Who could blame them?

I never got to see much else, because as the terror period was ending for the twins, so was my time in the Everglades. Lucinda would have to care for the house as well as the twins until the devils stole more slaves.

My New Home

I remember the last day in the Everglade house. The twins were doing much better. They'd lost a few pounds and had a slightly haggard look about them, but they were much more compliant. I was glad for their sake.

I began scrubbing the floors right after breakfast when Sally walked in.

"After you finish here, I want you to get cleaned up and put on your nicest clothes."

"Ma'am?" I asked. I know my surprise must have registered on my face. I looked up from my chore to see how closely she was watching me.

"Nick and I are going out, and we'll need your room. You're more than ready," Sally paused, waiting for her meaning to sink in. "You're going to meet your new family today."

They were going out today? That must mean... they were going to bring back more kids, and they needed my room. At last, I understood that my welcome had worn out.

My heart became a knife that began sawing my chest in half. My breath caught in my throat, constricting it, and threatened to close off completely.

I'd already lost my parents, and *now this evil woman was taking Lucinda from me?* I didn't know how to act or what to think.

While I was experiencing massive amounts of anxiety, Sally turned abruptly and left the room. I curled into a ball on the floor and tried to calm my nerves. I wanted to scream and throw a fit like the twins had done, but I knew that Sally and Nick would not be as kind to me as they were the younger children. Slowly, I recalled what Lucinda had instructed me to do to calm myself: I began giving myself math facts to compute.

When the fist clenching my lungs began to relax, I forced my hands back into scrubbing motions. Later, I mechanically showered and dressed. Then, I went to seek out my only support.

Lucinda was in my old room, reading the kids a book. They were on the floor. The little girl was curled in her lap while the boy sat beside her, leaning into her side.

"Okay, now we're going to clean up the room," Lucinda said as she closed the book. "That was a good story, wasn't it?"

My friend looked up and saw me in the doorway. She immediately lifted the girl from her lap and came to me.

"Zoey, what is it?" she asked. I could hear the worry in her tone.

"They – they're taking me away," I managed.

"When?" Lucinda's eyes were pools of worry.

"Now," boomed Sally's voice from behind me. "Say goodbye, then we'll be off."

We didn't need prodding. We grabbed at each other ferociously. I felt like an octopus, trying desperately to suction myself to my only lifeline. *What would I do without Lucinda? What would I become?*

"Oh, knock it off, girls," Sally commanded. She let out a huff of air. "You both knew this was a temporary arrangement. Hurry it up." She looked at her watch and said, "We need to go."

Was this woman really that unfeeling? I thought. *Was she that cold and callous that I couldn't even say a tearful farewell to the only person left in my life that I loved?*

"Can Lucinda come with us?" I asked softly. I knew my expression had to reflect my hopefulness.

"Absolutely not," Sally stated succinctly. "She needs to watch the twins. Besides, we need the space in the suburban as we will be bringing back more trainees. On top of that, there's too much risk. The twins haven't been here long enough to be trustworthy, so they can't come *or* stay by themselves."

"Couldn't I... help train?"

"It's already settled. I've been paid. Lucinda will have to be my main trainer."

Tears began streaming down my face. I felt wooden and unbending. I wasn't sure that I could move even if I wanted. Sally's eyes narrowed, and she grabbed my arm roughly and spun me away from my soul sister. I had to run with spread legs to keep myself from biting the floor. Even though I windmilled my arms, I still lost my balance and landed on my bottom.

"Get up and stop this silliness!" said the big drill master. A hint of anger laced her words. "Get in the car, and don't make me tell you again."

"Y – yes..." I hiccuped, "ma'am."

Lucinda's face looked as crushed as I was sure mine did, but neither of us had the power to stop our spiraling fate.

The twins chose that moment to begin squalling. Before Sally could make the situation worse, I turned and ran for the car. I could feel the tears burning trails down my cheeks.

The next few hours passed in a daze. I wasn't even sure how long I was in the vehicle or where we ended up. All I know is that we were still in the sunny state of Florida.

The suburban finally parked. I lifted my head and looked forlornly out the window. We were parked in a lot belonging to a huge supercenter department store. It was probably the largest one I'd ever seen, but then again, I hadn't seen very many.

Almost immediately, a sleek black Lexus pulled up next in the spot beside us. A couple got out and walked toward the suburban. They almost looked like brother and sister because their hair was an exact color match of light brown. They were nearly the same height. The man might've had an inch on the woman. Both also had the same type of body build; they were neither slender nor heavy. They didn't look out of shape or fit. They simply were.

Sally slowly got out of the vehicle as did Nick.

"Hello, there," Sally greeted. "You must be Ethan and Liz."

"And you must be Sally," Ethan returned. They both wore tight smiles on their faces.

"This is Nick. He's my partner in crime," Sally laughed dryly. "Zoey, come on out here," she commanded without waiting for a reaction.

I was shaking with fear. I knew Sally was bad to live with, but at least I knew what to expect and had Lucinda to love. These people just looked... uptight. At least Sally was relaxed. She was mean, but she was calm. These people didn't look like they ever took time to breathe. They seemed like the kind that flew one-hundred miles an hour until they slept. That gave me pause.

I tried to breathe in slowly, but my breathing was ragged. My hand was quivering so badly, I had trouble grasping the door handle.

"Zoey?" Sally's voice had an edge of impatience.

"C – coming," I said. My voice sounded as weak as I felt. Finally, the door creaked open, and I stumbled out.

Sally's eyes narrowed dangerously.

Five times six is thirty, I thought. Calming myself even more, I added, *At least Sally won't be able to punish me for acting scared.* That idea calmed me.

"H – hi," I offered shyly.

"Hello," the woman answered haughtily. She turned to Sally and asked, "She can cook and knows how to clean thoroughly?"

"Yes, ma'am. I guarantee it."

"She looks smaller... and scrawnier than the pictures. It makes me wonder."

"She's small but mighty. She'll work hard for you."

Liz said, "She should for the price you charge."

"You pay for what you get, and I'm the best," Sally replied with a warm smile and a wink. "I stand behind my product. She'll be scared at first, but then her training will kick in. She's very compliant. You'll be happy with your purchase."

"Good," the woman replied. Then she offered another tight smile and shook Sally's hand. Liz ignored Nick completely.

Ethan also shook her hand and nodded to Nick who mirrored his acknowledgement.

"Zoey, get in the car," the new woman said. Her words were sharp and staccato.

"Y – yes, ma'am," I stuttered. I opened the well-oiled door and sank into the plush back seat. I obediently buckled my seat belt. The new people talked to Sally a bit longer and then opened the doors simultaneously and settled in the luxury sedan.

When we arrived in the subdivision, I stared. The entire neighborhood was composed of huge homes with at least three or more car garages. They were lofty structures that no simple families would ever need. Each could hold a whole community of homeless people.

The residence we pulled in front of was grandiose. I'd never seen a house of such enormity. It was a three-level light yellow structure with peaks and mildly vaulted ceilings. An attached wing displayed three dormer windows on the top floor.

My heart dropped to my feet. I realized I was
going to be the one responsible for cleaning the
immense building. How could these... *people*...
expect a young girl to do the amount of work that this
would call for? Inwardly, I cringed.

The man, Ethan, pressed a button on the top of
his sun visor, and one of the many garage doors slid
up. He parked, and we got out.

"Follow me, Zoey," the woman said.

I shuffled after her and entered a small room
off the garage that had a bathroom and shower to the
side. Shoes of many assortments were lined up
against the wall.

"Take your shoes off here. I'll get you some
house shoes to wear," Liz informed me, "You won't be
needing normal shoes as you'll always be inside."

I bent my head and murmured, "Yes, ma'am."

We entered the elaborate kitchen. Shiny metal
appliances gleamed. Their cold images were mirrored
on the decoratively tiled floor. There was a breakfast
bar separating the large room from the equal sized
dining room. A cherry wood table was the
centerpiece where meals were served. A matching
curio cabinet with intricate carvings lit up fine china
from a nearby wall.

Frilly curtains decorated the
windows. However, the outside view was partially
obstructed by the thick, motorized shades. There was
a soft bubble pattern on the back of the filter.

"You'll be mostly working in this room to
start," Liz informed me. "I'll introduce you to our

daughters and then let you explore the kitchen to familiarize yourself with where things are located.”

“Yes, ma’am,” I said. I felt like those were the only two words I could say.

Ethan stood by the bar and waited while Liz went to retrieve their children. A short while later, I heard a muffled conversation and the front door opening and closing. Liz entered the room with two brown-haired girls. One looked roughly to be my age, and the other was approximately a few years older.

“Zoey, this is Brittany and Amber, our daughters. Amber is your age, and Brittany is a little older.”

“Hello,” I said shyly.

Amber replied, “Hi.” She flashed a wave at me.

Brittany, however, didn’t acknowledge my greeting.

“Mom, why is this girl here?” she asked. “I don’t wanna play with her.”

“Honey,” Liz answered, stooping to her level, “do you remember me telling you about a little girl who was going to come and clean for us? This is her. Zoey.”

“Oh! The slave girl?” Brittany said with a sneer. “Does this mean I don’t have to clean my room?”

Liz laughed. “You still have to keep it organized, but she will clean it when it gets dusty.”

“Can she clean it all the way for me, sometimes? Like put my clothes up for me?” Brittany pressed and wrinkled her nose.   "I hate putting up my clothes."

"Yes, I'm sure she can do that," Liz said.

Ethan just stood back and watched the exchanges.   His arms were folded across his chest.   He seemed to be assessing the situation to see how we all interacted, but it was hard to know for sure.   His face was an unreadable mask.

Gigi

"Remember, this is our secret," Liz cautioned. "You can't tell anyone at school that we have a slave girl living with us."

"Or anyone, anywhere," Ethan corrected. "If you do, we'll be in big trouble and then you will be. You'd have to go live with your poor cousins."

"Uncle Ajay?" Brittany asked.

Both of her parents nodded.

"NO!" she screamed.

"Yes," Ethan said, "you will. So, you can't tell *anyone*. If anyone notices her, she is your sister that has issues, so she has to be homeschooled, okay?"

Both girls nodded.

"But can we change her name?" Brittany asked, looking up at her mother.

"Well, I suppose," Liz agreed.

Ethan asked, "That actually is a good idea."

Liz looked at Brittany. "What would you want to call her?"

Brittany ran around the room like an airplane. Her arms were stretched out at angles, slightly behind, and out to the sides. She made zooming noises and ran two laps around the table.

"Well," she said when she finished her laps, "since you won't let me have a dog, I want to call her... Gigi."

Liz looked over at Ethan who nodded once.

"Gigi, it is," Liz agreed.

"Can she act like a dog, too? I mean, can she sleep on a doggie bed?" giggled Brittany.

"Sure," Liz smiled placatingly.

All I could do was stare, open-mouthed. Not only was I a slave, but now I was the equivalent of an animal to them? I was going to get to work hard and as a reward in this elaborate and expensive house, I *get to sleep on a dog bed?* I felt my lip tremble, and I nearly sat down and bawled.

"Ethan, after supper, how about I take the girls and go shopping for a nice big dog bed? If you could stay here with, um, Gigi, that would be great. I want to make sure to keep a close eye on her for quite a while."

"That'd be fine, hun," he acquiesced.

"What are we gonna eat for dinner, Mom?" Brittany asked.

"Can we have hot dogs and biscuits?" Amber asked.

"Now, when do we ever have hot dogs and biscuits?" Liz asked. "No, honey, I'm sorry. Pick something else."

"Chicken and dumplings!" Brittany said.

"I'll have to get some chicken," Liz said, "but we can have that tomorrow."

"Pizza?" asked Amber hopefully.

"I want to see what our new girl can do," Liz said. "I mean she could make home-made pizza, but I think of that as a carry-out meal."

"I think spaghetti sounds good," Ethan offered. "Let's not throw too hard of a meal at her while she's learning where everything is."

"Okay. That sounds good," Liz agreed. "Girls, is spaghetti okay for supper?"

"With cheesy bread?" Brittany asked.

"Of course," Ethan replied. "Spaghetti isn't spaghetti without toasted garlic-cheese bread."

Both girls nodded and then ran back out of the room. And as easily as that, I was dismissed from their attention.

I was actually grateful for a familiar chore. It gave me something to focus on besides my situation. I turned to begin the meal.

The kitchen was organized neatly and logically, so I had no problem finding everything I needed. In less than an hour, I had the table set and everything ready.

Ethan was working at the kitchen table to keep an eye on me. He moved all of his things right before I set it. He nodded in approval at my arrangement and food display.

"I'll go tell everyone the meal is ready," he stated.

I nodded slightly to acknowledge him. Then, I hovered nearby to wait on the family.

"Okay," Liz said after the first few bites. "I'm pleased so far with our purchase."

Ethan agreed.

"Mom, these meatballs are *better* than hot dogs and biscuits!" Amber said with her mouth full.

"You can say that again," Ethan laughed.

I poured milk refills as needed. After everyone was excused from the table, I was allowed to eat. There was plenty to fill me up, but the spaghetti was starting to get cold as the last clung to the sides of the glass serving bowl. There wasn't any bread left, but I knew better than to complain. The food was good, and I was full.

Liz and the girls came through the kitchen. Liz had a big purse slung over one shoulder.

"We're leaving now," she told Ethan. He nodded and looked back down at whatever he was doing.

I began cleaning. I noticed they had a dishwasher.

"Um, excuse me, sir?" I asked.

"What is it?" he asked, looking up from his paperwork.

"Do I... have permission to use... the dishwasher?"

"I'm not sure what Liz wants you to do," Ethan said. "Why don't you do them by hand tonight?"

I nodded and turned back to my work. I labored hard and did my best, partly because I wanted to try to impress my new family. I felt that, *maybe*, it might buy me a small level of respect. What I didn't know, however, is that I was really setting a standard of expectation. It didn't matter, though, because I always tried my best.

Staying busy was the only thing I was in control of. It was the only thing I had of accomplishment to show. I knew that my work and ethics were the only values tied to me in the world.

"I'm finished, sir," I offered a small curtsy to the man before me.

"It looks nice, Gigi," Ethan replied. "You may sit until Liz gets back."

I tried to look happy, but changing my name infuriated me. I was too scared to focus on my anger. I clenched my teeth but then sat at the table.

I didn't sit very long because it gave me too much time to think, so I explored the kitchen some more so that I knew where she kept pans, dishes, and spices. It was probably an hour later when they returned. I was in the walk-in room they called a pantry when I heard the door open.

"We're back!" Brittany announced. She skipped into the room.

I came to the doorway of the storage room to see what was going on.

"We got you a bed, Gigi," she said. She did a happy twirl. When her eyes met mine, they were slanted in a mean way, and she deliberately smiled with an upward chin tilt.

My heart sank. *What had I ever done to this girl to already be the brunt of her meanness?* She had everything, and I had a dog pad, so there was nothing for her to be envious over.

"Do you like your new bed?" Brittany asked. Her voice was full of false friendliness.

Brittany held up a thick, furry pad with Liz's help. It was for an enormous dog like a Saint Bernard or a Great Dane, but still. It was thin compared to a mattress. The spoiled girl was definitely rubbing it in because her grin widened as she watched my face.

I tried to mask my emotions, but it was impossible. A quick quiver or two from my chin increased her happy chatting.

"Where is Gigi going to sleep, Mom? I was thinking the basement is a perfect place for a dog."

"Hum," Liz said. "I want to make sure she behaves herself and doesn't try to run away or anything. That's so far from where the rest of us sleep."

"Please?" Brittany pleaded. "She can't sleep by me or Amber. Are you going to put her in *your* room?"

"Ethan?" Liz asked. "Could you install a lock on the laundry room door? That would be perfect. It even has a small bathroom off to the side."

"Are you sure? It's a little chilly down there at times."

"I'll give her some blankets."

He shrugged and said, "Very well."

Ethan got up and went to the garage. When he came back in, he had a few tools and some hardware. He disappeared downstairs.

"Amber, why don't you give her a tour upstairs while your father is working?" Liz suggested.

Amber said, "Okay, Mom."

My peer turned to me and said, "Come on, Gigi. There's a lot to see."

Meekly, I followed her. We climbed up the wide stairs. There was a rich deep carpet in the middle of the golden oak steps to keep one from slipping and to cushion bare feet. The banister was highly polished and had some fancy carvings on the border.

When we reached the top, Amber said, "This way."

I followed her over a broad catwalk that led to the dormered section of the house. The catwalk melted into an enormous playroom the two shared. The first door opened to Brittany's space. The room at the end was Amber's. Just their area was large enough for a whole house to fit in.

"The side over here," Amber informed, "is Mom and Dad's." She gestured to the hall at the top of the main stairwell back across the catwalk. When we got close, Amber pushed open the door

"Is it just a bedroom?" I asked.

"It's mostly their bedroom but the library is also up here," she said.

Bedroom was not a term I'd have used to describe where the couple slept. The main space looked like the entrance to a castle without the pointy parts. It was the very definition of extravagant.

In this section of the house, they had their bedroom and a bathroom with everything. There were his and her sinks, and they each had walk-in closets. A deep jacuzzi was next to a walk-in shower, and of course, there was a toilet.

Another door past the bedroom opened up into walls of books and plush furniture. A computer with a large display screen for anyone to use sat on an ornate desk.

I know I had to be moon-eyed while I took in all the exorbitant excess. I followed Amber back down the stairs. She proceeded to show me the main level. Besides the living room, dining room, and kitchen, there were two normal-sized bedrooms and a big office. Lastly, I was shown the basement.

The first room I entered was a second living room with a game room on the far side. There was a pool table and a few other games I wasn't familiar with. The format was open, so I could also see a section made into a home gym with Nautilus equipment, and some free weights.

An enormous guest room with a private bath waited to accommodate friends and family.

"There," Ethan said, wiping his hands on his pants. "All finished."

I froze. He was standing in front of a door by the home gym. I suddenly didn't feel like I could move.

Liz and Brittany came down the stairs, dragging the dog bed.

"Oh, you might as well come and see your room too, Gigi," Liz called.

It was a few moments before I could command my legs to follow. Finally, I managed to enter the laundry room.

The room was large. It held top-quality washing and drying machines. There were drying racks and bins for sorting clothes. In the corner, though, was my spot.

Liz or Brittany had placed the dog bed there. A few quilts were piled beside it along with a pillow on top. To be funny, I suppose, they also had a large stainless-steel dog bowl with a toy ball placed in the middle.

At least they didn't fill the vessel with water or dog food. I thought. Even thinking so, tears began to well in my eyes.

Distracting me, Liz said, "Your bathroom is in through this door. You have a toothbrush, toothpaste, a cup, a hairbrush, and a towel in there. I also put a few clothes we picked up for you on a shelf.

"After you earn our trust, I'll get you an alarm clock. Until then, you'll just have to wait until I get down here to get you up."

I couldn't talk past the lump in my throat, so I nodded.

"Well, good night then," Liz said.

Brittany bounced out and said, "Happy dreams, Gigi." She skipped over to me and patted the top of my head.

Finally, I was all alone. I might have been glad if the sound of the hardware jiggling hadn't killed any sliver of hope in my heart that I could lead a semi-normal life. My heart shattered into a million pieces in my chest, and I fell onto my bed with a sob and pressed my face into the pillow.

Oh, Lucinda. How I miss you. I would stay at Sally's forever if I could be with you. These new people are horrible.

<><><>

AGE NINE

I think I cried more than I had any other night except for those close to my initial abduction. Even at Sally's, I was treated respectably. I was human, at least. Now, I was a dog named Gigi. As a nine-year-old girl, I couldn't think of anything worse. *Happy birthday to me.*

I got up to use the bathroom and splash cool water on my swollen face. My head was screaming with pressure from my sinuses. I blew my nose then tried to lay back down on the memory foam cushion. It was cool in the basement, but when I covered up with the blankets, I was warm enough. The thin bed did help to protect against the coldness radiating up from the tiled floor, and it was surprisingly more comfortable than I'd imagined. I adjusted the pillow under my neck.

After a good cry with my misery, I was exhausted. It seemed I'd just closed my eyes when I heard the sound of the lock being rattled. My eyes popped open.

Liz came in and said, "I'll give you fifteen minutes. Then you need to come to the kitchen."

"Yes, ma'am," I croaked.

I blinked into the bright light a few times and rolled off my cushion. I stumbled toward the bathroom. When I looked back, Liz was gone. I let out a slow breath and gave myself a moment to pause.

Less than fifteen minutes later, I was standing in the kitchen. Liz handed me an apron to wear while I cooked.

"What would you girls like for breakfast this morning?"Liz asked her daughters in a sing-song voice.

"Pop Tarts," Amber said.

"We don't have any," Liz said patiently. "We have Gigi here, waiting for us to decide what she should prepare for a home-cooked meal. Now, what would you like for breakfast?"

"Cinnamon rolls," Brittany suggested with a wide grin.

"How about you offer them some choices, dear," Ethan suggested. "Then they will be on the same page as you."

Liz sighed. "Oh, I suppose you're right. We are going to have eggs, girls. How would you like them cooked?"

"Ewww," said Amber wrinkling her nose. "I don't like eggs."

"They're good for you, Pumpkin," her father said with a playful tweak of her nose.

"You can have an omelet, honey. That covers the taste of the egg up some," Liz said.

"No, it doesn't. Why can't we just have Pop Tarts?"

"You get what you get," Liz said. "And you don't throw a fit."

"Fine." Amber huffed out a sigh. "I guess I'll have an omelet. But put lots of cheese in it."

Ethan said, "I'll take the same."

Liz said, "I want mine scrambled with cheese and salsa." She looked at me when she said it. I nodded.

"Brittany, tell Gigi what kind of eggs to cook you."

"I want a fried egg sandwich with mayonnaise and mustard. Oh, and cheese, too." Her eyes darted to me, and she grinned.

"While you're at it, some bacon would be nice," Ethan added.

I nodded then opened up the cupboards to retrieve needed items. Numbly, I began cooking.

Flash Forward

Six years after my abduction:

AGE THIRTEEN

I often think back to the days when I was happy. That fateful day in Faery Tale Land was the best… and worst day in my life. That memory was six years ago; to date, I've never seen any of my family again.

While I reminisced, I felt a fat tear slide down my cheek. Finally, I shook my head and resumed washing the dishes. It was 1:00 in the morning. I would need to get some sleep before my day of rigor started all over again.

Normally, I had the dishes completed immediately after we ate, but tonight Liz insisted I prepare homemade bread that would be ready in time for breakfast, so I decided to wait until I was ready to wash all the dishes rather than do two batches.

I scrubbed the last pan and wiped down the kitchen. Finally, I clicked off the light and readied myself for bed. I placed my house shoes with my other pairs. I had a variety of styles, but no "regular" shoes. It was just another way Ethan and Liz showed how emotionally uninvested they are in me. After brushing my teeth and putting on my worn flannel gown, I headed to my assigned spot.

The laundry room floor was cold on my bare feet. I slipped on woolen socks and fell onto my bed. The large dog pillow crammed in the corner was more comfortable than the hard floor, but still, it wasn't the ideal place to sleep. Regardless, once my head touched the pillow, I was already nearly asleep. I curled under the two blankets I'd been issued and knew no more.

Early in the morning, at 5:00 a.m., my alarm woke me. Groggily, I rubbed my tired eyes. It was hard to drag my fatigued body out of my warm spot. I knew there would be consequences if I didn't, though.

I started a load of laundry and headed upstairs. I brewed a pot of coffee and began cracking eggs. The sausage was beginning to sizzle in the pan when I slid the biscuits into the heated oven.

In another forty minutes, the husband and wife would come down the stairs for breakfast. Usually on Tuesdays, I had sausage, scrambled eggs with cheese, biscuits, and gravy. Mostly the menu varied, but not on Tuesdays.

After the gravy was made, I began slicing large, succulent oranges in half. Then I squeezed all the juice out of them until a pitcher was brimming. Next, I set the table and organized the food items delicately around the new flower arrangement.

Finally, the couple was up. I heard the parents descending. They glanced at the table with the fragrant steaming food and barked an order.

"Go wake up the girls. I'm hungry." Liz sat heavily at the table. She rubbed her swollen abdomen.

"Yes, ma'am."

"I'm surprised you haven't done that yet," Ethan added. "Get me some coffee before you get them."

"Yes, sir."

I grabbed the coffee pot and poured him a cup full. I added the amount of cream he liked.

"None for me," said Liz. "But you can pour some orange juice while we wait on your inadequacy."

"Yes, ma'am," I said quietly.

"If you can't have your chores done before we wake up, you need to rise earlier," Ethan warned.

I spared him a glance of acknowledgement as I rushed off to get their children.

"Brittany," I crooned softly as I gently rubbed her arm. "Your parents want you to get up."

"Go away," she mumbled.

"Brittany, breakfast is ready. It's time to get up."

"You dumb *bitch*! I told you to go away!" She rolled over with a huff and covered her head with her pillow.

I sighed inwardly and went to Brittany's younger sister's room. Using the identical approach with Amber, I managed to wake her. While she dressed, I went back to her sibling's room.

"Brittany, please get up. Your parents are waiting for you downstairs."

"I said GET OUT OF HERE!"

I flipped on the light, resulting in a screech. I shut the door just as something hit the barrier. I returned to the kitchen.

"Sounds like Brittany's up," her father announced.

"What gave it away, Ethan?" his wife asked with a smile.

"She reminds me of you, Liz." Ethan's lips turned up in a smirk.

"That puts me in a good mood." Liz's tone was light and playful, but she tried to feign irritation.

Ethan chuckled. "Oh, you're not so bad... unless you're pregnant."

"Now whose fault is that?"

Ethan winked at his wife and said, "I don't know, but when I find the bastard..."

Liz got up and said, "Gigi, I want some food on all the plates when I get back down. It takes a real disciplinarian to get Brittany out of bed." She looked meaningfully at her husband. "I'll be right back."

Upon her return, her nearly seventeen-year-old daughter, with disheveled hair, plopped resentfully into her chair.

"Why do we always have to have this crap on Tuesdays?" Brittany griped. "Why can't it be pancakes or something good?"

"We have pancakes a lot," her father reminded. "This is what I like, and this is my day to choose what we have for breakfast. Eat up."

"Mom, I thought you said Gigi was going to make homemade bread?"

Liz turned to look at me with narrowed eyes.

"I did, ma'am." I gave a little curtsy. "Would you like me to place it on the table?"

"No, I had you stay up all night making it to leave it on the counter."

Heat flushed my cheeks as I scrambled to put a sliced loaf onto the already full table.

The family consumed their meal in relative silence. I waited on their every need. Afterwards, each individual went back to her respective room to prepare for the day. I began to clear the table.

I dished a biscuit and gravy onto my plate and a few of the scrambled eggs. Then I added a little strawberry jam to a small slice of homemade bread. I sat and ate quickly. Afterwards, I prepared a school lunch for the girls and loaded the dishwasher. I was scrubbing the pans when Brittany and Amber returned.

"Your lunches are on the counter," I called.

They both peered into their designer lunch bags.

"Mom!" Brittany yelled. "Why are you making us take lunches? You know I hate sandwiches!"

"They're healthier for you than school lunches," her mom called back.

"They SUCK!" Brittany made a face.

"I made your sandwiches with the home-made bread," I said, drying my hands on a kitchen towel.

Brittany ignored me. The two girls grabbed their things and headed out to their car. Brittany was allowed to drive to school one day a week, usually on Tuesdays. I guess Ethan didn't want to drive them to school on his special breakfast day.

"At least put something good in our lunches next time, Gigi," Brittany demanded. "Some chocolate or something."

"I can only put in what's available," I said.

I received a glare as the girls slammed the door with their departure.

"Instead of being a smart ass, clean this kitchen," Liz said. "I'm going upstairs for a bit." She pressed a hand into the small of her back.

I glanced around at the already-clean kitchen but said, "Yes, ma'am."

The kitchen was immaculate when the married couple came back down. Liz handed me a list.

"We're going out for the rest of the day. I want all these chores done before our return. Do *not* break any of the rules while we're gone," she warned.

"Yes, ma'am," I said, bowing my head.

"We have eyes watching," Ethan reminded.

I took the list and tried not to sigh. It was going to be a long day.

My Eighteenth Birthday

My eyes opened in the dark. It was midnight and officially my birthday. It was not a joyous occasion, though. This day haunts me every year... for ten years and counting. The love and acceptance given by the gift of family, taken for granted by childhood innocence, had been tossed recklessly aside. Oh, what I wouldn't do to have the chance to go back in time to relive that day.

They say hindsight is 20/20, but mine was better than that. Now, instead of happiness, togetherness, cake, and presents, I was just a work horse sleeping on the laundry room floor with a dog's name. At eighteen, I should have received the gift of freedom from the shackles of childhood.

I shook my head and sighed. It was time to stop feeling sorry for myself. Normally, I tried not to dwell on my misery, but the thoughts, memories, and yearnings couldn't always be kept at bay. My birthdays were the days I struggled with the most.

My dog bed was thin now and very uncomfortable. The hardness of the tile under the flimsy layer was becoming harder to ignore. At eighteen, my body was athletic and strong from the years of manual labor, but I still ached from such a poor sleeping arrangement. I also was a lot larger than I had been at nine.

I stood and stretched for several minutes. Then I pulled on my too-big shirt and cheap leggings. The house shoes I had were a little too small and worn, but they would do. After brushing my teeth, I headed upstairs. I tied the apron around my waist.

I readied a breakfast casserole with sausage, mushrooms, tomatoes, onions, and spinach. When I popped it in the oven to bake, I made Angel Rolls, a simple and easy recipe that everyone seemed to love. They didn't need preparation from the night before and were quick.

About fifteen minutes before the meal was cooked, I put on a fresh pot of coffee and carefully set out the dinnerware. Because Liz insisted on an elegant table, I had to clean and starch the tablecloth frequently. I was very careful not to spill anything on it.

When the family came down for sustenance, the kitchen was sparkling clean and smelling divine.

"Wow, everything is so beautiful," Amber said. Her widened eyes gazed around the table. "It's white and sparkly. Great job, Gigi."

"She must know today is the day we're going to plan your birthday celebration," Liz said. She looked at me and gave a small, tight smile.

"But my birthday isn't for two weeks," Amber said. She looked a bit confused.

"All the better to plan. If we don't think about things now, we won't have time to get them done."

"Oh, okay," Amber said. "Well, Mom, it's not like I'm a little kid anymore. I don't need an actual birthday party. Save that for Ashton. I'll probably just go hang with my friends."

Liz buckled the happy four-year-old toddler into his booster seat. Ashton picked up his spoon and banged it against the tray.

Liz looked at Amber and said, "Gigi, here, needs to bake you a cake. You can at least plan to spend time with your family on your birthday. Then you can go out with your friends."

"Sure. Well, I like cherry cheesecake. Or ice cream cake. I don't like real cake that much. That buttercream icing is just too rich."

"Let's plan on New York-style cherry cheesecake." Liz glanced at me.

"Sure, Mom," Amber said.

They all sat down at the table, and I passed out slices of the casserole with Angel rolls to each person. I poured milk, orange juice, or coffee to each one as well. Then, I stood quietly, ready to refill each glass or plate as needed.

Half way through the breakfast, Amber said, "Hey, Mom? When is Gigi's birthday?   I know we're about the same age."

"I'm not sure, honey. I'm not sure if Gigi even knows," Liz replied. "And besides, I know you're at least three years older than her."

"What?" Amber asked. Her fork froze, suspended halfway to her mouth. "I *know* she's my age."

"Not according to the papers I received from Sally," Liz laughed. "And we know those documents are the *real* deal."

"Mom." Amber's fork clattered onto her plate. Her brows crunched down in disapproval.

Brittany grinned. "She certainly *acts* fifteen. Maybe someday, when I have a family, I'll give good ole' Sally a call," she laughed harshly, and her eyes slid over to me while they talked.

"You better have a gob of money saved," Ethan said.

"Gigi, you're my age, aren't you?" Amber asked, ignoring her family's cruelty.

I could only nod.

"Do you know more, Gigi?" Amber asked. "Do you know when your birthday is?"

A huge lump formed in my throat, so I nodded again.

"When is it, Gigi?" Liz's gray-brown eyes seemed to dare me to answer. "When... is your birthday?"

I stood against the counter and opened and closed my mouth a few times. I simply couldn't make my voice respond.

Amber looked at me. She must have noticed I was close to tears. "Gigi? Are you okay?"

For the first time since I'd lived with them, I tore out of the room and ran for my corner. I nearly fell down the stairs in my haste to escape.

It was too much. In this family, I felt the closest to Amber only because she'd never been mean to me, but she was still one of *them*. I knew that meant I couldn't trust her.

Since it was my birthday and I was reliving pain through the loss of my family on that wonderful-horrible day, I just couldn't talk about it. The devastation was still too raw.

I fully expected the sound of feet running down the stairs to force me to return to my huge amount of chores, but I was left in peace for about an hour. When I reemerged to the kitchen to clean, everyone had left for the day.

I supposed my "gift" was less chores than normal and to be left in peace.   For that, I was thankful.

Mr. Ponder

A few months after Amber's birthday, I'd just finished cleaning the kitchen when Liz came down the stairs shortly after the girls left for school. Her brows were pressed down over her eyes, and a downward tilt was pasted to her lips. Ashton was perched on her hip.

"Gigi, I'm going out with Ashton. Ethan won't be home until this afternoon."

I looked up because she expected it. I figured she had a play date to occupy the energetic youngster, but I wasn't allowed to ask.

"I posted a list of chores on the refrigerator. You're to have them done before we return."

"Yes, ma'am," I said.

After they'd gone, I looked at the list. It was a lengthy one. I had to mop and scrub the floor and trim, dust the ceilings and fans, polish all the furniture, and dust everything on all three levels. In addition, I had to have the evening meal prepared by 6:00 and do three additional loads of laundry which included folding and putting away. I growled in frustration. It was an unrealistic list. Vaguely, I wondered what I'd done to displease Liz.

No matter how long the list was, the first thing I was going to do was go for a walk. I wasn't allowed outside, but I was going to go anyway. What they didn't know wouldn't hurt them.

I loved to feel the sun on my skin, even if it was getting cold. Just a walk around the block couldn't hurt. Then I'd dive into the work assigned. If I had time, I'd sneak into Liz's library and try to read a few pages of a book in there, too. I loved to learn, but I wasn't allowed to attend school.

I snapped up a discarded jacket that I kept in my area for nights that got too cold for just the blankets, and I put on hand-me-down sneakers. Once outside, I set out at a quick clip. I relished the sting of cold against my skin. It made me feel alive and that there was more to life than my current situation.

When I turned the corner on our block, I stopped. I tilted my face up to the sun. I closed my eyes and felt the brightness through my lids. A slight chilly breeze kissed my skin. I smiled as a burst of appreciation for the simple beauty of the day overtook me. I held my arms out at my side and slowly turned in a circle a few times. Then, I began to walk once more.

Our neighborhood was elegant. Mostly, it was filled with wealthy families that all worked during the day. It was the safest time for me to venture outside without being seen.

When I got back home, I began my impossible chore list. I set an alarm to remind myself when to start supper. I began with the upstairs. It took me two and a half hours to thoroughly clean all the bedrooms and the bathrooms. When I was half-way through the main floor, the alarm to begin supper sounded. I was far behind where the Mistress would want me to be. I had done a fine job, so I hoped that she would be satisfied with me completing the remaining floors on the morrow, but deep down, I knew she wouldn't be.

I began frying the premium pork chops. I cut asparagus spears, drizzled olive oil over them, then seasoned them with garlic salt, a dash of mixed seasonings in a shaker, chili powder, and pepper. I'd bake them when the meat was a little closer.

Next, I boiled potatoes for homemade mashed potatoes and gravy. Fresh rolls were ready for the baking sheets as well. I planned to drizzle seasoned butter on the steamy tops before setting them on the table.

When the family was seated and served, I relaxed a little. So far, each person seemed to be in decent moods. It wasn't until after I began clearing the plates that Liz spoke.

"How did the chore list go, Gigi?"

It was like she already knew. Maybe she'd set me up for failure on purpose.

I gave a little curtsy to show my respect. "I'm sorry, ma'am, but I only got the top floor completed and part of the main floor before I needed to cook your supper."

Liz's face clouded over. Her brows rumpled over her eyes, and her nostrils flared. "Let me get this right," her tone was frozen. "You've had *all* day to work, and you only got the top floor completely finished?" Her sneer sliced my heart. I knew this meant no mercy.

"I'm sorry, ma'am. I did a very thorough job, and I couldn't do a good job cooking if I'd have continued cleaning."

"Well, clean the kitchen and get to work! You'll need a few hours of sleep before breakfast in the morning. I expect pancakes – unburned – when we come to eat."

"Yes, ma'am."

I mechanically began cleaning the kitchen. I needed the time to prepare myself mentally for my long night ahead. I suppressed the need to cry; it wouldn't do any good. I took a breath and remembered the simple pleasure of the walk and realized that I'd have done it all over again. That made the work a little easier to bear.

I was grimy and filthy many hours later. I was too exhausted to even wash up. I knew dirt and cobwebs were on my clothing, and probably on my face as well, but at this point, I didn't care. I'd only have an hour and a half to sleep before the alarm sounded. I curled up on my dog bed, and like a light, I was out.

The next morning, I took a warm wash rag and tried to wipe my face, arms, and hair so I wouldn't look so grimy before cooking. I didn't have time to shower, but I knew Liz wouldn't be forgiving if I looked dirty while cooking for them.

I dragged myself up the stairs to start the coffee brewing and to prepare the pancake mix.

Liz was pissed. It showed from the day's equally long chore list. I supposed this was an additional punishment. Usually the lists were long, but not so long as to be impossible.

I silently fumed. Since my addition to this family, I'd basically been a slave. I'd learned to cook and clean thoroughly. During my training, if you want to call it that, if I didn't do a good job, I didn't get to eat until I did. I was quick to learn their expectations. I also don't get to go to school because Liz was afraid I'd tell someone about being stolen or how they treated me.

Liz was normally the last of the family to leave the house. On this particular morning, an unexpected knock resounded through the foyer. My authority figure looked at me with surprise registering on her face. She walked to the door and looked through the peep. Then she turned to me and frantically gestured to make myself scarce.

I knew the command meant that I was to become invisible: she didn't want to see, hear, or think about me. But that was going to be impossible...

"Hello, Mrs. Chancellor," a man's voice greeted.

"Good day, er... Mr...." Liz leaned closer to stare at the man's identification tag attached to his lapel, "...Ponder."

The man at the door was of average height and had thinning brown hair and a matching mustache. He wore a blue suit and striped tie.

He asked, "May I come in?"

"What is this pertaining to?" Liz did not offer to move aside.

"The young lady in this house." Mr. Ponder craned his neck to see around Liz.

"My daughters are at school."

"I'm speaking about the one that isn't." The man's patience was evident in his tone.

Liz shifted her weight and said, "I'm sorry, but I don't know what you're talking about."

"Mrs. Chancellor. I know there's a young lady in there, right now. If you don't let me in to talk with her, I'm afraid I will have to take more drastic measures."

"I want to know what the Division of Family Services has to do with me!" Liz declared angrily. "I pay my taxes, and I'm not abusive! You have no right to question me." Her grip tightened on the door until her knuckles were nearly white.

"I'm sorry, ma'am, but every time we have a hotline situation, we *are* obligated to check it out."

Liz sucked in a noisy breath. "*Hotlined*?" she exclaimed, her tone incredulous. "I. was. *HOTLINED*?"

"Yes, ma'am," Mr. Ponder replied calmly.

"WHO HOTLINED ME?"

"We are not at liberty to disclose that, ma'am. Many times, our hotline callers remain anonymous." Mr. Ponder's voice was the same measure and tempo as when he'd first knocked on the door, but one could tell he was not a push-over.

"This is simply ridiculous."

Mr. Ponder gave her a minute more to process the situation. Finally he asked, "Ma'am, are you going to let me in?"

Liz replied tersely, "I'm not happy about this but I suppose."

Liz opened the door slightly wider to allow him access. The man in the crisp business suit walked in. He smiled disarmingly at Liz and walked slowly around the living area. His eyes seemed to miss nothing. Eventually, he arrived at the kitchen table and sat.

"What are you doing?" Liz asked, appalled at the man's seemingly rudeness.

"I'm going to wait here until the young lady presents herself."

Liz stood, rooted to her spot. She swallowed, but afterwards, her throat continued to work. Finally, she forced words out.

"You are quite pompous, aren't you?" she asked foully.

"I usually get what I come for," the man returned. His lips slowly reflected a gentle smile.

Liz sighed and strode forcefully from the room. She rounded the corner and saw me standing just out of sight from the dining room. She grabbed my arm in a vise-grip.

"You better toe the line," she hissed in my ear, "or I'll see to it your brother disappears, and he won't have the princess accommodations you do, Gigi. Lie if you have to but make that man happy and go away."

I could sense the fear in Liz, and in reaction, I could feel my eyes grow larger. I swallowed hard and whispered, "Yes, ma'am."

Slowly, I walked into the dining room. I looked at the floor shyly.

"Hello, young lady."

"Hello," I offered. I glanced up at him and then away again. I *was* a bit nervous, so it wasn't all an act.

"I'm Mr. Ponder," he said, walking over and offering me his hand.

"I'm… Gigi," I said, shaking his hand.

"Well, Gigi, I'm going to get right to the point." He waited until I looked up at him. "Why aren't you in school?"

I quickly broke eye contact and studied the floor. My toe moved in a circle on the clean surface. "Because… ah, well, um, because… I'm homeschooled."

"Why aren't your… sisters?…homeschooled then, as well?"

Even though I didn't glance up, I could feel the heat of his gaze on my shoulders.

"Because… I'm… shy. I don't like going to school. It makes me have too much anxiety, and then I fail…" I lied. "My sisters… don't have my problems."

In the corner of my eye, I saw Mr. Ponder cross his arms. "Please show me a recent homeschool test, or I'll need to give you one to make sure your education is appropriate for your age."

"What? Please don't give me a test!" I gasped. "I get really bad anxiety!" I wrung my hands for effect.

Mr. Ponder dropped his arms and said softly, "Look, Gigi. I have to have proof. Either I need to see a test today, or I need to come back."

My eyes darted to his face. "Um, please come back?" I shrugged helplessly.

Liz moved from the entrance of the dining room toward the kitchen. She was looking at me murderously.

"Mrs. Chancellor?" Mr. Ponder inquired. When he looked up, she quickly assumed a pleasant look.

"Yes?" She ripped her eyes from mine and studied Mr. Ponder. Her eyes held a charge of defiance.

"Can your... er, daughter... read?" He met her challenge and played the trump card.

"Of course, she can read!" Liz's tone was indignant.

"I want to set up a test to assess her knowledge."

"*WHAT*?" Liz's body seemed to freeze. A look of near horror was etched on her features.

"I would like to test Gigi," the middle-aged gentleman repeated.

"What for?" Liz's pallor had whitened, but she was already recovering.

"It's good for all homeschooled children to be evaluated to see if the curriculum is suitable for that student's needs," Mr. Ponder said.

"Even if they're learning disabled?" Liz asked with a tiny smile uplifting the edges of her lips.

My head snapped to look at her before I could hide my reaction to her words. If Mr. Ponder noticed my response, he covered it well.

"Even the mentally-challenged children must take assessment tests for the state near the end of every school year," Mr. Ponder said. "I can tell just by talking to Gigi that if she indeed has a disability, she is perfectly capable of taking a test in the privacy of her own home.”

“Fine,” Liz barked. “Make an appointment.” Her fisted hands rested on her hips. She moved toward the dishes in the dish rack.

“In one week, then, Mrs. Chancellor, I’ll be back. You did bring up an interesting topic, though. I’ll need to set up two appointments for testing. If she has a learning disability, first, we’ll need an IQ score. Then we can assess her actual performance levels.”

She half-turned to look at him.

Mr. Ponder’s attention was already back on me. “Exactly how old are you, Gigi? It makes a difference on which IQ test we give.”

I could feel Liz’s heavy gaze on me, daring me to say something out of line.

“I - I’m, um, fifteen.” I looked down and rubbed my hands together.

Mr. Ponder nodded. “Gigi? I’d like to visit with you a little longer,” he announced, then looked pointedly at Liz.

Liz turned to the dry dishes and began putting them up. I nearly gasped at this unusual behavior, but recovered as realization dawned on me.

“Excuse me, Mrs. Chancellor?” Mr. Ponder raised his voice so he could be heard over the clatter of dishes. When he once again had Liz’s attention, he said, “Either direct us to another spot where I can speak privately to Gigi, or pause in your chores for a bit of time?”

Liz's cheeks brightened angrily.   Her lips were pursed in a tight white line.   She said, "Stay in here.   I'll be in the other room." Liz turned and strode angrily from the adjoining rooms.

Almost without meaning to, my ears strained to hear her eavesdropping at the door.

Mr. Ponder walked to the sparkling kitchen table and pulled out a chair for me.   I hesitated, so he nodded at me with a reassuring smile and said, "Please, sit."

I slowly approached and sat in the chair.   Mr. Ponder took the one beside me, but he made sure he respected my personal space.

"Okay, Miss Gigi.   How long would you say that you've lived with the Chancellors?"

I looked up, searching for what to say.   Finally, I said, "I'm not sure, Mr. Ponder."

He nodded once and said, "Take a stab in the dark."

"Um..." I looked up as if thinking about it.   "I guess maybe about nine years or so."

His brows raised. "Is that right?" he said. His eyes seemed to pierce into my resolve.   "And have you ever attended school while in this home?"

I shook my head again. "No, sir."

Mr. Ponder's voice lowered.   "*Are* you homeschooling?"

I wondered briefly if he also believed that Liz was trying to hear our conversation.

"Yes, sir," but I'm sure he noticed my eyes dart away to mask the deception of my statement.

Mr. Ponder leaned back a little. I felt him looking at me again. Finally, he asked, "And about how long do your chores take you a day?"

I looked back in surprise, reading the knowledge on his face. I could feel my mouth open slightly in surprise, so I quickly closed it. I gasped shakily, "Just a few hours, sir."

Once again, the suited man's brows raised. He leaned a little toward me. "Are you sure about that, Gigi?" he asked quietly.

I looked down again but nodded. I didn't trust my voice at the moment.

Mr. Ponder said quietly, "Look. You can shoot it straight with me. I won't tell."

He noted the barely perceptible shake of my head. I took in a soft slow breath. Mr. Ponder didn't say anything for a few minutes. Finally, he asked, "What are they hanging over your head?"

I wisely said nothing. I didn't trust my voice or my actions. A tiny tremor rattled my backbone, and I felt as if time were standing still.

Here was an opportunity to set myself free, a chance of a lifetime... *my* lifetime, but the years of living in fear held me imprisoned. I knew Sally could reach my brother if anything was revealed.

Mr. Ponder sighed softly and said, "Okay, Gigi. I won't force anything on you, but if you ever want to talk, here's my card," he said and pushed a card with his information into my hand. I slid it into my pocket before he stood and called for Liz's return.

Liz made a dramatization of returning into the kitchen as if she had been far from the room when Mr. Ponder called her.

Mr. Ponder didn't react to her grand entrance. He waited patiently until she appeared ready to listen.

"I'll be back next Wednesday," Mr. Ponder informed. "I want to see all her legal paperwork then. In addition, I'll bring the intelligence test."

Liz said, "I don't suppose I have a choice."

"Not really, ma'am. Good day," Mr. Ponder said with a slight smile. He patted my back as he walked by me to let himself out.

As soon as he drove away, Liz turned on me with fury blazing. "HOW did he know you're here?" she barked.

I could feel myself shrinking back from her. "I – I don't know, ma'am!"

"*Somehow*, someone has seen you!" she hissed. She clutched my arm in a vise-like grip.

Her talons bit into the tender flesh on the inside of my arm. Although I really wasn't sorry, I bowed my head and whispered in the most shamed voice I could muster, "I'm sorry, ma'am."

"You better be." She abruptly let go and gave me a little push. "Now finish up your work!" She shoved me again, but this time, she meant business.

Quickly, I made for the door. Just before I pushed through, I heard Liz call after me, "Gigi?"

I paused. "Yes, ma'am?"

Liz looked me up and down. Her brows created a worry line over her eyes. "You, um, *can* read?"

"I haven't been given any books to read," I confirmed, "but I can read some."

Changes

The next week passed in a blur. I was a nervous wreck, but I managed to talk myself out of several panic attacks. When Mr. Ponder appeared at the appointed time, my apprehension wasn't a pretense.

"Are you ready, young lady?" he asked after settling into his chair across from me.

I drew in a deep breath and swallowed audibly.

"Look," he consoled. "This is just an intelligence test. It measures your ability to learn. You can't fail."

"Really? I thought it was an academic-type test."

"We'll get to that. Your, *ahem*, mother said you had a learning disability. In order to determine this, we need to test your IQ. Then we'll do an academic test."

"Today?"

"No, I won't do that to you. I'll make another appointment for that, tomorrow or the next day."

I visibly relaxed. When we'd finished, Mr. Ponder dismissed me so he could talk to Liz. She was sullen and nearly noncompliant. The only reason she cooperated was to keep further involvement at bay.

I went to the living room and sat on the couch as Liz had instructed me to do while Mr. Ponder was there.

I couldn't hear what they were discussing, but soon, Mr. Ponder followed Liz out of the kitchen.

"Show me Gigi's bedroom now," he instructed.

Liz led the way to the end of the hall. She opened the last door on the left to the smallest room in the house.   Considering the size of the home, the room was still large comparatively.

"This is where Gigi sleeps?" asked Mr. Ponder.

"Yes."

"This reminds me of a guest room. Where are all her belongings?"

"Um, she actually donated a lot of it to charity.   She likes to give to the needy."   An uncomfortable silence stretched before Liz hastily added, "But I promised we'd go shopping tomorrow to get her more appropriate wear."

I heard a satisfied noise of acceptance from Mr. Ponder.   "I want to see her room again upon my return."

When the DFS agent left, I resumed my work.

"Gigi?" Liz asked, struggling to keep the anger out of her tone.

"Yes, ma'am?"

"After the girls are off to school tomorrow, I'm going to take you to get a few things."

"Oh, thank you, ma'am!" I said, struggling to keep the excitement out of my tone.   I really hadn't been out of this house except for my little escape walks.

Liz took in a slow breath. "And you're to sleep in that room now."   She barely flicked her hand in the direction of the hall toward the smaller of the two guest rooms. I could tell it took a lot for her to issue those words.

"Oh, thank you!"   I couldn't believe my good fortune.

"You are not to talk about your life here," Liz warned. "If you continue to keep up your chores, you may have one hour to study a day."

"Oh, thank you, ma'am!" It felt like that was all I could say.

"Just do your best on that damn test."

That night, for the first time in nine years, I slipped into the warmth and comfort of a real bed. It was only a twin, but it was luxury like I'd never imagined. The soft mattress enveloped me in a cloud of warmth, and the sheets were of the softest fiber. I rubbed my cheek on my pillow, enjoying the silky feel on my skin. The comforter was light and airy but was warmer than I'd have thought possible. I snuggled in deep for a wonderful night's sleep.

The next morning, I woke up earlier than usual. I smiled and stretched as I looked around the room. Although it was the smallest room in the house, I was happy. It was the largest space I'd had in forever to call my own.

I was so excited about my upcoming excursion. I was allowed to get out of my jail to go shopping.

I made an elaborate breakfast. Everyone was pleased. I even put extra good things in Brittany and Amber's lunches.

"After I see a spotless kitchen, we can go," Liz stated.

"Yes, ma'am," I replied, already setting to work. I smiled when I saw my ratty old dog bed in the pile for Ethan to take up to the trash dumpster.

About an hour later, I sat in the back seat. Liz wouldn't allow me the privilege of sitting beside her. I'm sure she thought that would make me feel more like an equal.

Liz took me to an upscale second-hand store. I was fine with that. The clothes inside were nicer than I'd ever had. I was allowed to select one modest dress, two pairs of jeans, a few sweatpants, tees, a lightweight jacket, and one coat. In addition, I got a few sleeping ensembles and a fluffy robe. I also got to pick out a newer pair of tennis shoes and a pair of fashion boots to go with the dress. Try as I might, I couldn't entirely wipe the happy smile away.

Finally, I'd graduated from animal status into the human domain.

When we got back home, I began all my chores. I even hummed as I worked. I felt rejuvenated. I actually had my *own* room and clothes. Wow.

That evening, I was so exhausted. The excitement from the day and the full-time work had worn me out. I couldn't wait to crawl back into my real bed.

The next day, Liz had me move everything out of the nursery. She wanted to transform the nursery into a toddler's room, so I taped the trim and put plastic down. Between layers of blue paint, I performed my normally expected chores.

"Now," stated Liz, "this room is fit for a toddler growing into a boy."

When I finally got my hour off, I found myself dozing until the loud entrance of Brittany and Amber startled me.

"Hey, Mom?" Brittany called. "Can Blake come over?" she asked hopefully.

"Yes, but only for a few hours."

"Will you make Gigi clean my room?"

"Sure, but he's not going in there."

"Come on, Mom! I'm an adult! I'm twenty and in college now."

"Not going to happen. My house, my rules."

Brittany saw me trying to study. "You heard mom. Go clean my room."

When I looked at Liz, her commanding stare was obvious. So much for my one-hour break.

Internally, I was fuming. At least my anger gave me the energy needed to tackle the task. I still felt appreciation for having my own things, so my anger was short-lived.

Right when I'd settled back down over my book, Brittany said, "Mom, make Gigi clean Amber's room, too. I don't want Blake to see it like it is."

When I'd finished with the rooms, it was time to start the family dinner. I was told to set an extra place at the table.

"Mom, will you make Gigi wear a maid's uniform for when Blake is here?" She giggled.

"No."

"Awww, why not?" Brittany crossed her arms over her chest and pouted her lips.

"Because I don't need another report of Gigi not being treated decently."

"But we *do* treat her decently," Brittany laughed and glared at me.

"Are you or your sister wearing maid uniforms?" Liz asked.

"Heck, no!"

"See? For anyone who asks, we all take turns making dinners," Liz said.

"Even though we don't?" Brittany laughed again.

"Even though we don't," Liz confirmed. She nodded and smiled.

"Fine."

Inside, I was furious, but I dared not show it outwardly. I would continue serving this family until I could figure out something new. The Chicken Alfredo was slightly simmering when the visitor arrived. I added a splash of lemon and a little more cream.

Brittany was all a flutter. She gave him a tour of the house.

"You have a very nice home," Blake said when they'd taken their spots at the table in the formal dining room.

"Thank you," Brittany replied.

Time lapsed as each thought of a new topic to discuss.

Finally, Blake asked, "Who's that girl in the kitchen?"

"Uh, she's... part of our family."

"Really? She seems... different."

"Ya, she's our adopted sister."

"How come I've never seen her before?"

"She's shy, and so she's homeschooled."

I purposely tuned out of the conversation. I was highly uncomfortable with the obvious distinction between the family and me, so I poured myself into my work, and the rest of the evening became a blur.

Never before had I felt so isolated. As soon as I was able, I melted into the background. Then, after chores, I went to my room.

I made sure to keep repeating my real name in my head when I was alone. I was no longer a dog to these people, but neither was I human. I was still just a slave, never to be equal in their eyes.

At times, I revisited my past. I reserved part of myself for the memory of who I used to be and of the family I continued to love and miss. It took practice to recall the faces of my mom, dad, and brother. My memories were now more of the essence of who they were rather than individual features. At times, I still cried myself to sleep. Tonight was one of these nights.

Normally, I'm not the kind of person to wallow in self-pity, but even the young man who'd just met me knew I didn't really fit in. The recent joy of my shopping excursion diminished in my sadness, but I continued to try to hold on to it. It would forever bring me happiness to think of that moment of semi-freedom; it was the most I'd had in ten years.

The next morning, I wondered vaguely about Mr. Ponder and when he'd be back to discuss my academic testing. As promised, he'd returned a few days after my IQ test, and I'd taken different subtests for most of the afternoon.

As I cooked the morning meal, I thought about it. I knew my education was quite a bit behind, but I was still excited to find out how I did.

Almost as if on cue, the doorbell rang. Liz answered the summons. The family had just sat down to enjoy breakfast. Ashton happily made a mess in his booster seat.

"Oh, look! Mr. Ponder!" Liz announced loudly.

"Sit down with a plate of food and eat with us," instructed Ethan. "Now!" his terse command was softly uttered.

I scrambled to fill my plate and obediently sat. I ate a few bites to look as if I also had been enjoying my meal.

"If you don't mind," Liz began, "wait in here until we finish our family meal."

"I just would like to peek in the kitchen for a second to say hi to Gigi, and then, of course," Mr. Ponder replied, unruffled.

Honestly, I knew Mr. Ponder just wanted to see if I was getting to eat or if I was just doing all the work. Oh, how I wished I could tell him how it really was.

"Hello, Gigi," Mr. Ponder greeted me. He waved.

"Good morning, sir," I replied, giving a small wave back.

"Not to ignore everyone else, good morning, all." Mr. Ponder's brown eyes landed on each person. "I'll be waiting in the living room," he said.

The atmosphere of the breakfast changed. Everyone seemed to eat as quickly as possible then the girls left for the day. While Liz cleaned her son, I cleared the table and set all the dishes in the sink for washing after our guest left.

"Mr. Ponder," Liz called. "Won't you join us?"

When the DFS agent entered the room, Liz introduced him to Ethan.

"Gigi, did anyone help you clear the dishes?" Mr. Ponder asked as he settled at the freshly cleaned table.

Ethan's eyes widened at the question, but the man's attention was on me as I joined the gathering at the table.

"Um, Mr. Ponder, I usually do the dishes in the morning because my sisters attend school. I have time where they don't." I tried not to look at the Chancellors as I rehearsed my line.

"I hear you're here to discuss Gigi's academic results with us?" Ethan asked.

"Yes, sir, I'll be discussing her performance and her potential. If I may, I'd like to start off by saying that Gigi's intelligence is excellent!"

I beamed at him.

"Gigi, an IQ score that is considered normal is 100," he explained. "Yours is 123, a very nice score."

"Thank you, Mr. Ponder."

He nodded then continued. "Gigi, this is not directed toward you, understand?" At my nod, he said, "It's quite disturbing to see Gigi's academic levels when compared to her potential to learn." Mr. Ponder gave an accusatory look at my *parents*. "It's almost as if Gigi's really had no training past fourth grade, and she should be a sophomore, or, at the very least, a freshman by age fifteen."

"How dare you!" Liz exploded. "I told you already that she has a learning disability."

"Now, darling," Ethan said, calmly pulling her back down. "Let's hear him out."

Begrudgingly, Liz sat. It didn't stop her eyes from shooting daggers.

"A true learning disability can't be from lack of educational opportunity," Mr. Ponder replied, "and since you can't supply any given tests or give the name of the curriculum you're using, I have to think that's the reason." The DFS worker paused. "This means she does not have a true disability."

I could sense the accusation in the air, and I think the Chancellors did, too.

He looked directly at Ethan and Liz. "I know you've stated that Gigi is adopted, but here's the thing: her file is missing. It seems there isn't any real paper trail to follow."

"*What*?"

"The agency said that a fire wiped out their history including computer files, but it's deeply disturbing that there's no documented proof that Gigi is here legally. I'll need to take another look at your paperwork."

"Um, sir? Just what are you implying?" asked Ethan. His face was reddening. "We showed you our documentation. I don't understand why you need to follow up."

"Just what I've said," Mr. Ponder replied. "You have no way to prove that you adopted Gigi through legal channels. There is not a trace of paperwork at the agency.   Therefore, by the power of the state, I've opened an investigation."

"AN INVESTIGATION OF WHAT?" Both of my guardians leaped to their feet.

"A hotline call was initiated, and if I'm suspicious, which I am, that there is not equitable and just treatment of your, *ahem, adopted* daughter to your legitimate daughters, then I will open a case to determine if the treatment is actually fair and appropriate. In simple terms, I suspect emotional abuse or neglect."

"This is simply ridiculous!" Ethan yelled angrily. "She is healthy and provided for. How dare you!" His words reflected his wife's earlier outburst.

"If you can't control your reactions, I can have the child in question removed from your residence and placed into foster care while the investigation is underway."

I noticed an immediate change in my guardians' demeanors. They certainly didn't want me leaving my prison and their supervision. Then, they wouldn't be able to control my explanations and reactions.

"What does this mean? Please explain... this case?" Liz haltingly asked. Her throat worked at swallowing, and her eyes still gleamed with rage.

"It means I'm not satisfied with your explanation as to why Gigi stays at home and works nonstop for this family to the point that her education is sacrificed while your biological children have freedom, privileges, and a life, as well as the social aspects of a formalized educational setting. This is not fair and equitable in the least. I gave you the benefit of the doubt, but all my suspicions were confirmed with the level of performance on Gigi's test in relation to her abilities."

I sat quietly at the table, doing my best not to fidget. Ashton toddled over to me and raised his hands. Happy to have something to occupy myself, I picked him up.

"And furthermore, it's obvious to me that you're holding something over this child's head," Mr. Ponder nodded slightly in my direction.

"She is not a child," Liz argued.

Ethan roared, "Like WHAT?"

"Search me," Mr. Ponder said. "All I know is that this young lady deserves, and is going to get, a lot more. Because you are so very vague with what regularity that Gigi sits down to study, I'm at liberty to require a tutor. If you choose one, I must approve. I can appoint one for you if you don't have someone in mind. You need to set up tutoring sessions three times a week. I suggest on Mondays, Wednesdays, and Fridays until Gigi is caught up with her education. I also recommend finding a curriculum very soon. I'll need the name of the program."

"B – bu – but," Liz stammered, "Didn't you say she was *years* behind?"

"That I did. But lucky for you, she's fifteen. It won't be long before she's a legal adult where we have no say in her education. At that time, we'll get her signed up for programs to assist her if you decide you don't want to help her out... that is unless you say she's still welcome to live under your roof."

The rest of the conversation and visit passed in a haze for me. *I was going to get a tutor.* Socialization with people beyond this particular family. I nearly swooned with delight. Maybe… just maybe I could start to fit in somewhere.

When Mr. Ponder left, Ethan and Liz began a heated discussion. I quickly put Ashton down and got to work. I rinsed the dishes and put them in the dishwasher. I began scrubbing the pots and pans. Still, I couldn't block out their words.

I heard Liz yell, "So how are we going to keep her forever when he knows about her? Are we going to have to move?"

"I'm not giving up all we've worked so hard to achieve."

"Ethan, we could go to *jail* if Gigi decides to tattle."

"I know that, Liz. She won't." I could feel both of their heated gazes on my back. Ethan continued loudly, "She cares about her brother too much."

Liz was quiet for a few minutes.

"And we'll get to keep her," Ethan's voice said calmly.

"How do you figure?"

"DFS only cares about minors. Once she's seventeen or eighteen in their records, they won't lift a finger to help."

Another moment of silence.

"I suppose you're right," Liz sighed loudly. "This is just so stressful. Maybe I should have told him she's eighteen."

"It's too late now. We've got to stick with what the paperwork says."

"True." A few minutes later, Liz was irate again. "But that's three damn years of this shit!"

"Liz, Ashton."

The toddler was beginning to cry.

I started the dishwasher and left to begin other chores. I saw Liz swoop up her son and pat his back as he hugged her. *Love and acceptance must be nice.*

My Tutor

That evening, I served the meal. I made Baked Tilapia flavored with spices, dill, and lemon, served over a bed of rice. Salad complemented. For dessert, I placed a large baking pan full of chocolate chip cookies in the oven.

As I poured Brittany's milk, she looked at me.

"I hope you made a great dessert, Gigi. I'm not on a diet."

"I think it's a good meal," Amber said, forking some fish into her mouth.

Liz finished chewing a bite when she turned to Brittany.

"Brittany, does your college offer any tutoring services?"

"I, um, I'm not sure. We have a few places we can go to different help centers. I'll check it out. If they don't, I know I can find one. College students always need a few extra bucks. I can help Amber if she needs it."

"It's not for Amber."

Brittany's eyes slid over to me, and her mouth dropped open. "You're kidding."

"Unfortunately not. Do you remember me telling you about the man from the Division of Family Services? He tested Gigi and told me in no uncertain terms to hire a tutor. And he has to approve my choice. Can you believe such nonsense?" Liz's voice was starting to raise.

Ethan patted her. "Hon, no sense in getting worked up again. Do what you've gotta do. The sooner we comply, the sooner the man will be out of our hair."

"Let's hope."

"Sure, Mom. I'll find a tutor to come to the house. What are you willing to pay?"

"Make it a dollar or two better than the going rate?"

"Fair enough." Brittany bit into a chocolate chip cookie and closed her eyes for a moment.

"Brittany, not to rush, but if you could find one within the week, that'd be great."

"You bet."

A few days later, Brittany came home and handed Liz a torn piece of paper with a number scrawled across it.

"What's this?" Liz asked.

"It's a name I got off the wall advertising a tutor-for-hire. I asked around, and he comes well recommended."

"Do you know him?"

"Never met him, but he should be able to help," Brittany said. "Give him a call, Mom. Working on such a low level will be easy money for him. I'm sure he'll jump at the chance."

I turned my back to those sitting at the table so they wouldn't see my shame. I knew I was smart. Mr. Ponder gave me that. I listened to everything I could, the television, the radio, and those around me. I also taught myself when I had a chance. Still, the

Chancellors loved to put me down, and just the fact that I needed a tutor didn't help my self-esteem.

"After you finish up your evening chores," Liz said, "Sit at the table and do some studying. The new curriculum books just came in today."

"Yes, ma'am," I said. I rushed from the room to finish up the laundry. Anything to get away from those judging expressions.

At about nine that night, I sat down. I pulled out a literature book. Brittany walked by and sneered, "Do you need help reading? That word is *the*."

I knew better than to make the remark I wanted, so I just shook my head. "I'll figure it out."

She snorted and left the room.

I forced my attention to the story. It was intriguing. It was called "The Lady or the Tiger?" I likened the princess in the story to Brittany. If they were anything alike, I knew for a fact that her lover was a meal for a tiger.

All too soon, my eyelids were drooping, and I couldn't focus. I dragged myself up and prepared for bed.

Time flew by. I was waiting nervously for my tutor to show, so when the doorbell rang, I nearly had a heart attack. Liz opened the door, and in walked the agent from the Division of Family Services. He smiled at Liz then focused on me.

"Hello, Gigi," said Mr. Ponder.

"Mr. Ponder. Are... you going to be my tutor?" I asked. I hoped my face didn't register my disappointment.

"Oh no, my dear. I'm here to meet and approve the coach."

"Okay." I took in a deep breath and let it out slowly.

Liz didn't say anything to either of us. About five minutes ticked by, but to me, it seemed like five hours. Finally, the door chimed.

Liz smoothed her skirt and opened the door. A very attractive young man entered the room. The first thing I noticed was his stunning royal blue eyes. His crisp dark brown hair bordered on black and was a striking contrast.

Even Liz seemed stunned. She stood, frozen, for a full two beats before regaining her cool composure.

I didn't recover quite as quickly. My mouth dropped in shock, and I froze. He was the most handsome man I'd ever seen. Surely, he wasn't here to see *me*. For a moment, I felt like I couldn't breathe.

The young man flashed a smile at both Liz and me. His teeth almost seemed to dazzle.

Liz was also taken aback by the man's attractiveness. She seemed to be stammering and moving things around that didn't require it. Then, the curtain on the stage dropped when she realized this guy was here for me.

She gave the young man a generous smile and said, "I'm Liz Chancellor, and you must be Chance, the tutor."

"I certainly hope to be," he said. His voice was a warm tenor. When he met Liz's gaze, her eyes seemed to flutter in reaction.

The agent stepped forward. "Hello, Chance. I'm Mr. Ponder. We'd like to ask you a few questions if you don't mind?"

Liz's face whitened, and her lips compressed into a thin line.

"Sure, Mr. Ponder. I expect as much."

"This young lady is Gigi. She's who you'll be working with."

"Hello, Gigi. I'm Chance. It's nice to meet you." He walked to me and reached out a hand. It was strong and lean looking with nice clean fingers. I tentatively held out mine in greeting. He shook my hand and held it a little longer than necessary.

I peeked up at him. His height made me feel very feminine. Chance's vibrant eyes were concentrated on me. He watched as I studied his features. His dimples deepened when I blushed. His proximity made me unsure, and I took a small step back.

"Um, hello," I returned finally.

Mr. Ponder asked, "Mrs. Chancellor, where would you like us to informally interview this young man?"

"We might as well go to the dining room table."

I turned and followed Liz. When we settled down at the table, I was across from Mr. Ponder with Chance on my right and Liz to my left.

"How much experience have you had tutoring?" Mr. Ponder asked.

"This is my second year doing it for money," Chance said. "I also donate a bit of time to a nearby district. I did a practicum there, and I loved it so much that I sometimes just go there to help."

"What is your major?" Liz asked.

"Undecided, right now. I'm interested in biology and psychology, but I enjoy all sciences. I've thought about teaching or maybe even counseling, but I'm leaning more towards pediatrics."

"Are you a sophomore or a junior?" Liz asked.

"It's my second year in college, but I'm technically a junior. I'll be going a lot longer if I decide to go the medical or psychological routes, though."

Mr Ponder nodded. "Are you a decent instructor in all areas? We're looking for someone to help Gigi in every subject: English, algebra, history, and science. A few side assignments of fine and practical arts would be great additions."

"I'd like to say so, Mr. Ponder. I have references from all age groups and grades I can provide, if you'd like."

"Yes, please."

"What is your rate?" Liz asked.

"Twenty an hour."

"I'll call a few of your references," Liz said, "but my daughter who goes to the same college, asked around about you, and we liked what we heard. If that's the case, I'll pay twenty-five."

"We'd like to see how you work with Gigi," Mr. Ponder said. "We'll want her opinion, and then we can decide if you're the right fit."

"Fair enough."

"Gigi is behind in her studies," Liz said. "So it will seem as if you're instructing someone younger than she. I just want you to know ahead of time so you won't be shocked."

I shrunk down a little in my chair.

Mr. Ponder turned to Chance and wove his fingers together in front of him before resting them on the table. "It seems that she's had a lack of opportunity rather than ability," he said.

I had to give him credit. His eyes never flickered to Liz.

"I'll get you caught up in no time," Chance said. "Now, don't you worry."

The intensity of those blue orbs looking at me was powerful. All I could do was nod.

"Thank you, Mr. Ponder. Mrs. Chancellor," Chance said, "I'll take my leave and let you discuss this further."

"Wait just a moment, young man. Let's go ahead and set up your trial. Mrs. Chancellor, would Tuesday afternoon work for you?"

Liz looked at her phone and said, "Yes, that would be fine."

Chance said, "Good. I'll see you then. Bye, Gigi."

"Bye," I called softly.

"I'll be back on Tuesday to see how the trial run goes," Mr. Ponder said, standing.

After they left, I threw myself into my work. Liz was angry, and I knew it was best to stay out of her way. At dinner, she complained because she needed to vent, but she also wanted me to hear what she had to say.

"That awful man from the DFS ran the entire interview today," she steamed.

"Stand up to him, dear," Ethan said.

"Oh, believe me, I'd love to. I'm just afraid that I'll go nuts on him if the door cracks open too widely. I mean, he acts like it's *his* decision on whether we hire the guy or not!" she huffed angrily as she took a bite of the creamy potato soup and cornbread I'd made. "I mean, is *he* going to pay?"

"Well, what did you think of him? The, uh, tutor."

Liz had a far-away look in her eye. "Oh, he's very... capable... it sounds like. I just don't know if Gigi can handle it."

"What do you mean?"

"He's quite attractive. I think she'll make a fool of herself."

I dropped the ladle in the sink.   It clanged noisily before I could sweep it back up. All heads swung toward me.

"I - I'm sorry. I didn't mean to."

"Clumsy girl," Ethan muttered. He looked back at his wife. "What makes you say that, hon?"

"That right there." She pointed at me by the sink. "Plus, her being around a guy? Working in close proximity? I just don't like it."

"You can shop around more," Ethan said. Then he laughed out loud. "Maybe you should put out an ad. I don't know. You could say, "Tutor wanted. Must be knowledgeable and ugly.""

Liz's face reddened. "Oh, knock it off."

Ethan pressed, "Or maybe ask for a woman tutor only?"

"How cute is he, Mom?" Brittany asked.

"To die for. He looks like he could have a career in the movies."

"Oh, really?" Ethan asked, raising a brow.

"Really," Liz said with a smug smile.

"When's he coming back?" Brittany asked. "I wanna see what he looks like."

Liz's face clouded. "In a few days. I need to call a few of his references first."

"I just might need some tutoring sessions," Brittany said with a wink.

I resumed my duties and tuned them out.

Tuesday couldn't come fast enough, but I was a little worried about working with a man so closely. I knew Liz would watch me like a hawk, but that wasn't really my concern. She always watched me closely.

When I laid down that night, I thought about tutoring and what the sessions might be like. I knew Chance was just another person, but his attractiveness made me nervous... well, it made me self-conscious. I was embarrassed to be so far behind in my studies, and for some reason, what he thought about me mattered. And sitting so close to such a handsome male? I swallowed so loud I heard it clearly.

Finally, Tuesday arrived. I was a nervous wreck. I prepared a simple breakfast because I was worried I'd burn something.   I smoothed my hair and tried to hum a melody to distract myself.

"Oh, knock it off already," Liz said. "You're even making me nervous. Take a deep breath and try to learn something, okay?"

"Yes, ma'am," I said.

The doorbell rang. Liz let Chance in. I stood quietly except I didn't seem to be able to stop moving my hands.

"Hello, Mrs. Chancellor. Hello, Gigi."

Liz gave a smile and nod.

"H - hi, Chance," I said.

We stood there, looking at each other for a bit.

Liz said, "Well, come in the dining room and have a seat at the table.   I think that is the best place for tutoring sessions."

"Yes, ma'am," Chance said in his pleasing tenor.

As we walked toward the kitchen, the bell rang again, and Liz let in Mr. Ponder. Liz poured cups of coffee, and they talked quietly. They leaned on the bar between the rooms so they wouldn't disturb us.

Once seated, Chance began, "Let's start with a free program on-line. It's a neat database that allows you to read things at your own level and quizzes you over the selections. You'll begin with a pre-test to establish a beginning point. Then, based on each quiz performance, the next selection assigned takes into consideration how well you scored on the one prior."

"Okay."

The next half hour I spent reading several stories and quizzing over them.   It was extremely difficult to concentrate with Mr. Handsome over there.   He worked on something on his computer rather than observing me; I'm sure he understood how it would make me feel to be watched.

Next, we worked on math. I was decent at life-type of math, but not so great at geometry. Chance reassured me in his warm and pleasing voice.

Our time together passed by very quickly. Before he left, Chance gave me work to do before he returned. I was happy he did, because Liz would actually have to give me time to get it done now. There's one thing I know about Liz: she wants to look good.

"If they approve me, I'll be back in a couple of days, Gigi," Chance's voice interrupted my thoughts. "I think we're going to make great progress."

I flushed and looked down.

"Hey," he said. "We have a great start. Getting you caught up will go faster than you might think."

I didn't know quite what to say, so I nodded. I'd actually never been given any social opportunities since I was eight. How was I supposed to act? I mean, the guy was devastatingly handsome. I've had little experience with people in general, but with men? Zero, none!

After he left, Mr. Ponder said, "I think that went well. How do you feel, Gigi? Are you comfortable working with Chance?"

I fidgeted. "Yes, sir. I'm just not confident when doing school work."

"Maybe a woman tutor would be better," Liz suggested. "That guy is nice and all but maybe she won't make as much progress if she's so nervous."

My face must have said it all because Mr. Ponder ignored Liz and sat down by me.

"Gigi, do you feel comfortable with me?"

"Yes, sir."

"Now, you would tell me if you were uncomfortable working with that young man, wouldn't you?"

"Yes, sir. I like him very much. It's just... I'm sure I won't feel comfortable with *anyone*, but I'm excited to learn."

"Very good. It's settled, then. Right, Mrs. Chancellor?"

Through gritted teeth, she agreed.

Learning

When Mr. Ponder left, I put on my work clothes and got started. Liz was acting a bit strange. She kept huffing and putting things down harder than necessary. I kept quiet, doing my best to shrink into the background. I didn't want to ask her any questions. I was pretty sure I knew what was bothering her.

That evening at the dinner table, Ethan looked up at me.

"Dinner is very good, young lady. I'd like you to make this more often, please." He put another forkful of the creamy spinach, garlic, and Parmesan orzo with crispy bacon in his mouth.

"Yes, sir."

His attention shifted to his wife. "How did today's tutoring session go?"

"Well, it'd go a whole lot better if that *man* wasn't here," Liz grumbled.

"Ponder?"

"Of course. There's no changing tutors since *she* likes him," she said with a toss of her head my way.

"It is irritating indeed," Ethan agreed. "Just look at it as if we're jumping through hoops. Cuz that's what we're doing at this point."

"I know, Ethan. That man is just so insufferable. Truly."

Ethan gave a tiny smile. "I have faith in you, dear."

Brittany said, "I'm showing up next time. I gotta see what this guy looks like."

Liz smiled at her daughter and nodded. I cleared the dirty dinner plates and set out smaller clean plates. Then I retrieved a banana pudding for their enjoyment.

Two days later, I sat at the dining room table preparing for Chance. I was still nervous, but at least the worst was over. Nervous, I could handle. Anxiety was another story.

I put my completed work neatly next to the spot he used. I even completed a few of the extra reading quizzes online when Liz gave me permission to use the laptop. I set out bottles of water then went into the living room to sit. Finally, the door rang. Liz opened the door and moved aside to let Chance inside.

He smiled at Liz and greeted us warmly. "Hi, Gigi. How did it go? Did you have any trouble completing your homework?"

"Not really," I said. "I put what I completed next to where you sit. I also did a few extra quizzes online."

"Great! I like motivated learners."

He led the way to the dining room. We assumed our seats, and I opened the laptop while he looked over my work. Liz sat at the table and pulled out a book. I noticed Chance glancing at her while he perused the papers.

"Nice job," he said. "Did you have any questions about any of this?"

"Not yet," I said. "I'm sure I will eventually."

"Okay, great. Let's get started."

We worked on all four subjects, but we spent the most time on English. About a half hour before we wrapped up, Brittany walked in the door from the garage. She gave a delicate giggle then said, "Oh, hello."

"Hi, darling," Liz said with a wide smile.

"Who's this?" Brittany asked.

"Brittany, dear, this is the young man who's tutoring Gigi.   He's the one you found at your college. Chance, Brittany. Brittany, Chance."

Brittany batted her false eyelashes and walked to the table. I tried not to grit my teeth as I noticed the exaggerated swing of her hips. Chance watched her approach. She smiled, and her red lipstick seemed to make her teeth look brighter. They matched the stark white fitted shirt over stylish jeans.

"Nice to meet you, Brittany. So, um, you go to the same college?" Chance said with a returned smile.

"Yes, it's my second year," she said.

"I appreciate the help getting this job. Working with such a smart young lady is quite a privilege." Chance's rich blue eyes slid over to me.

I could feel a little heat rising to my face and looked down, but not before I caught a slight frown on Brittany's mouth.

"If I need some help on my algebra, would you be able to help me?" she asked, leaning in a little closer. "I wouldn't need *near* the help that Gigi does, but maybe just a little?"

Chance met her gaze. "Of course. Just let me know when you'd like to set it up."

She smiled prettily. "Maybe next Tuesday, in about a week? Right now I have a B in the class, but I want an A."

"Sure, but we'll have to do Monday or Wednesday. I'm not here on Tuesdays."

"Monday, it is." Brittany smiled and batted her eyes before walking away.

We finished up my session, but I was sure Chance could tell a difference in my demeanor.

Right after the handsome tutor left, Brittany waltzed over to her mother.

"Oh, my *god*, Mom, He's *hot*!"

"I told you so."

"He's even hotter than I imagined. *YUM*!"

Liz laughed at her daughter while I was growing angry. I rarely ever said a cross word, but I couldn't help myself.

"Brittany, don't you already have a boyfriend?"

Surprise widened their eyes, then both sets narrowed as the full focus of their attention settled on me.

"You wait a minute here," Liz barked. "You don't EVER talk to my daughter with that tone! Do I make myself clear?"

Before I could utter a response, Brittany said, "*Yeah*, Gigi! Even if I have a boyfriend, I still have a pulse!"

They turned back to each other, giggling like children.

"Oh Lord," Liz said. She dramatically waved her face with her hands.

Brittany said, "Anyway, I'm not locked into any one man. Maybe I'll just trade up." A wicked grin spread across her face.

I stood quickly. I was sure there was some work somewhere in the house that needed my attention. Anywhere but the rooms they were in. As I passed, I could feel their satisfied stares on my back.

For the next few days, I threw myself into my chores, and when I wasn't slaving away, I dove into my studies. I didn't have to hide my learning anymore, and I was excited to grow. I couldn't wait to show Chance all I'd accomplished. He was due to show up at 10:30.

Directly after I cleaned the kitchen after breakfast, Liz instructed me to make chocolate chip cookies.

"Ma'am, may I make them after my tutoring session?"

"No, you may make them right now. If you're worried about getting dirty, put on an apron."

"Yes, ma'am."

I finished baking and cleaning the kitchen for a second time about twenty minutes before the tutor's arrival.

When Chance rang the bell, Liz brought him to the table. She'd sat out a glass and a platter of the warm cookies.

"Would you like some milk, Chance? I thought you might enjoy a snack while you work with Gigi. Something to break up the monotony."

"Thank you, Mrs. Chancellor. That's very kind of you. Working with your daughter is a pleasure."

He bit into the chocolate chip cookie and made a low rumble deep in his throat. "These are very good."

Liz smiled and looked at me. "I wanted to do something nice for all your time here. It didn't take long to whip up a batch."

"Thank you, ma'am. Gigi, did you try one?"

Liz smiled and put a glass of milk in front of me, too, then settled at the table with her book.

I couldn't stop from glancing over at Liz. She was watching me from over the top of her story. When our eyes met, she gave me a Cheshire grin and returned her attention to the book.

I felt a gentle pressure on my arm. Rather than speak, Chance had gained my attention by touch. When I looked up into those rich eyes, I could tell he'd seen the exchange between Liz and me. I swallowed.

"Um, what do you want to start on first?" I asked. I noticed my voice had a tiny temor.

He looked at me a moment longer before pulling out a math paper. "Let's begin here, today."

When Chance left, I got straight to work. Even Liz couldn't find a flaw with my efforts. I poured myself into my studies, and found myself in a wonderful world of knowledge and stories. It was the happiest I'd been in some time if the fleeting thoughts of my brother didn't pop up.

I worried about Chance noticing Liz's spitefulness. *Would he suspect anything? If he did, what would that mean?* I worked harder to keep myself from overthinking.

Friday's tutoring session arrived. I sat at the table, reading a story when I heard Liz let Chance in. I glanced up and saw a slow smile spread across his handsome face as he walked toward me. Liz trailed and sat at her usual spot at the table.

"How did it go these last few days?" Chance asked.

"I feel that it's going great."

Chance laughed. "That's an understatement. You've gone up two and a half grade levels with a week of reading."

"I love to read," I said. "That's the easy part. My struggle is more science, and math is getting to be a challenge."

"Those are more in-depth subjects," Chance agreed. "It'll come, but it'll probably be a little slower than with your reading jumps," he grinned.

Liz shifted and looked at both of us. "Wait until you work with Brittany," she said.

A flash of surprise lit Chance's face momentarily, but he recovered quickly.

"I look forward to meeting with her, Mrs. Chancellor. Next time, right?"

"Yes, on Monday."

"Very good."

I could feel my face harden. Every bit of joy I experienced had to be countered with a move by the Chancellors.

"Um, will you sit with us when I instruct Brittany as well?" Chance's royal blue eyes focused on Liz.

My brows shot up, and my eyes darted to Liz. By the expression on her face, she was caught off-guard.   I could see the wheels turning in her mind as she processed the question.   If she sat with Brittany, she would freak out. It had to appear that she was treating us equally, so it wouldn't make sense that she sat with me.

"You know, you're right.   I just wanted to make sure that Gigi was... comfortable... meeting a new person and working closely... with you. She has *significant* anxiety."

Chance turned to me. "Gigi, do I make you uncomfortable?"

My eyes flashed toward Liz and back again. "Um, no?"

Chance looked back to Liz. "I can understand your concern, Mrs. Chancellor, especially at first, but I think Gigi is comfortable learning with me now."

"Are you saying you don't prefer me sitting with you?" Liz pasted a smile on her lips.

"No, ma'am. But sometimes, the pupil does a little better if there's a bit of distance from the parent in the learning environment. It's not for me to say if that applies here or not."

Liz's emotions paraded across her face. I could see her realization of the trap she created for herself by asking Chance to also tutor Brittany.   Now her treatment of both of us would have to be more equitable.   I smiled inwardly because I knew the only option she had was to give us more space, or she'd increase Chance's suspicion.

Liz sighed and pushed back from the table. "Gigi, I'll see how it goes. You let me know if you start to feel any anxiety." The look she gave me held a bit of a warning.

"Yes, ma'am," I replied.

Chance took out a page in science, and we began to discuss what mistakes I'd made as Liz slowly walked away.

"You have a fairly good sense of biology," Chance said. "We'll work on learning the phases of cell reproduction. I want you to study over the weekend, and I'll give you a small test over it on Monday. How does that sound?"

I nodded.

"Hey, if you're too nervous, I can postpone the quiz."

"It's... not that."

"Are you upset because I'll be working with Brittany?" he guessed. His voice had lowered in volume.

I couldn't answer at first. I swallowed hard. I didn't want him to think I was jealous, and I didn't know what to say. I didn't know him well enough to even be jealous. It was more that the Chancellors were stealing away something that I felt was mine. The only thing I had. Again.

"Hey," he said softly. He took a finger, bent it, and hooked it under my chin. He gently lifted it until I looked up at him. "What's going on, Gigi? You can talk to me."

I nodded. "Um, thank you, Chance."

"For?"

"Saying what you did to Liz."

"Oh, sure. I can see something's going on between you two, and I knew you'd be more comfortable if she'd back off a bit."

I nodded. *He had no idea.*

"Do you... want to talk about... anything?" he asked. "Like... why does Mrs. Chancellor try to push your buttons?"

"I - I can't."

I could feel his warm gaze on me, but he finally let it go.

"Okay, then, do you feel like working on analysis in literature?"

"Sure."

"Let's discuss 'The Most Dangerous Game'. It's a popular story in curricula across the country, so it's one I want you to be familiar with. Identify the parts of a plot at the end, and we'll discuss more of the literary elements as we cross them. You have enough silent reading on-line. I want you to read this to me. I'll pause you when necessary. Some of the words may be a challenge. That's what I want to see."

"Okay."

In the middle of our discussion, Liz wandered in to grab a glass of tea from the refrigerator. She looked over at us and asked, "How's it going?"

"It's going really well, Mrs. Chancellor."

She looked pointedly at me.

"Yes, ma'am," I quickly responded. "Chance is a very good tutor. I'm learning so much."

Liz's mouth tightened fleetingly before it was replaced with a smile.

"Good. How much longer will your session be? It's nearly time to wrap it up, isn't it?"

"Yes, ma'am," Chance replied. "I just want to finish our literary elements discussion so Gigi can study for an upcoming test . She'll have a quiz in biology next time, then English the time after that. Her progress is phenomenal."

Liz nodded, took a drink of her tea, then swept out of the room.

A Glimpse of Humanity

As soon as Chance left, Liz was on me.

"You think you can get away with a little alone time, huh?" Liz yelled.

"I - I was just working on school work."

"I saw how you were scooting closer to him. You best not say a word about anything. I mean nothing about *NOTHING*."

"I won't, ma'am. I wouldn't do that."

"You better not. I'll make your life a living hell if I even get a glimpse of you trying to whisper anything to him. Do you understand?"

I nodded, and I could feel the tears swimming in my eyes.

"It would have been best if you told him you have too much anxiety to work with him without me there, but I suppose it's too late for that." Her brows bunched over her grayish-brown eyes, and she propped her fists on her hips.

I looked down. I didn't think I could say anything at the moment.

Liz went to the fridge and pulled out porterhouse steaks and two hot dogs.

"I want you to grill these to perfection," Liz said, slightly lifting the packaged steaks. "You know how we like it. Mine, medium. Ethan likes his on the rare side but not too rare. Brittany the same. Amber will take hers medium-well. You will eat the hot dogs. Cook them any way you like. Use the grill off the balcony."

"Ma'am, excuse me," I began. "You've, uh, never let me use the grill before. I wasn't permitted to go outside, so Ethan always did that. I, uh, don't know how."

"Well, you're going to learn, and you better not burn these steaks. Ethan will show you how to operate the grill. You know how to use a meat thermometer. For now, get on the computer and find instructional videos if you need instruction on how to grill. Do that now, and I'll sit for a few moments."

"Yes, ma'am," I said.

I pulled the laptop closer to me. I fought back my anxiety. Liz's actions reminded me of Sally and how she treated me when I was first learning how to cook.

"You will also make baked potatoes and saute some mushrooms to top the steaks. There's also fresh corn on the cob. Prepare that as well. You can choose our dessert."

"Yes, ma'am." More nerves welled in my throat, so I took in a deep but quiet breath, then released it slowly. I typed in grilling videos and watched a few before retrieving the potatoes.

Ethan looked up at me as he cut into his steak. "Is it my imagination, or are you getting better and better with cooking?" He patted his belly for emphasis. "I think I've put on a few pounds lately."

"Um, *my* steak is too done," Brittany said with a glare.

"It's the same temperature as recommended on the chart I found," I said. "The same temperature as your father's. Maybe you need it more on the rare side then, next time?"

"I know the correct terminology of how I like my steaks," Brittany said. Her lip curled in a sneer. "Just admit it. You messed up."

"Mine is just a tad rare," Liz said. "But overall, you did okay for your first time."

Amber said, "Gigi, mine is amazing. Brittany just likes to complain. I'm sure you already knew that, though." She glared at her sister.

"How do you know?" Brittany said. "Did you take a bite of my steak or something?"

Ignoring her, Amber said, "Mom, you need to treat Gigi better. I mean, making her eat hot dogs when we're eating Porterhouses? And she always cooks so well."

"Amber, Gigi is treated well enough. She has a warm bed, a roof over her head, and plenty to eat."

Amber shook her head. "It just doesn't seem right the way you all treat her." She put a bite of steak in her mouth. No one said anything even though they'd paused from eating. Amber, knowing all eyes were on her, sliced off a sizable portion of her steak and put it on a clean plate. She placed it at the spot where I'd sit when it was my turn to eat.

"Here, Gigi. Take some of my steak. I'll share with you. You don't have to give me any of your hot dogs in return, though." She looked directly at her mother when she said it.

The silence continued to stretch. I began topping glasses for something to do.

"It wouldn't hurt her to sit down and eat now," Ethan said. "I mean, basically, all our needs are fulfilled."

Liz glared at him. "You, too?"

"Liz, it's not like she hasn't already waited on us. She's not going to take anything for granted. I think it would be good for her to sit down and begin eating at this point in our meals. Go ahead, Gigi. Have a seat."

I looked back and forth between Liz and Ethan. Two at the table were shooting daggers at me while the other two had eased expressions.

Slowly, I pulled out a chair and sank into it. When I put a potato and corn on my plate, Brittany suddenly stood.

"I'm done. I can't eat this crap," she said, staring down at the tender cut of meat. She shoved in the chair and stomped from the room. Liz just stared after her. She opened her mouth once, as if to call out, but then shut it.

Amber reached out a hand and touched my arm. "Just ignore her, Gigi. You know how she likes to be the center of attention. Go ahead. Eat."

With a nod from Ethan and no words from Liz, I took my first bite.

Over the weekend, I did my best to stay out of Liz's sight while cleaning. I knew she wasn't really on board with my new step up into the world of humanity.

For the next few meals, Brittany didn't eat with us. She grabbed something and left without any goodbyes to her family or stayed in her room.

While I was cleaning the baseboards of the living room, I overheard Liz complaining to Ethan. They were watching television and weren't really paying attention to me.

"You're actually choosing *Gigi* over our daughter, Ethan?"

"No, Liz." Ethan sighed. "Brittany is too spoiled. She's an adult now and will move out some day. It's time we started to give Gigi a little more respect. She has grown into a wonderful servant. We don't pay her aside from providing for her. It's time that she earns a bit of a break, don't you think? Let Brittany throw her fits. We have another daughter to think about, and Amber doesn't think how we treat Gigi is right. Respect both of our daughters."

Liz slammed down something and said with a sigh, "Very well."

I heard the couch rustle as Ethan shifted weight. I imagined him leaning in closer to his wife.

"We've got to walk a careful line, Hon. Amber is just as important as Brittany. Just because she doesn't throw hissy fits doesn't mean her opinion doesn't matter. We certainly don't want her to complain to anyone."

The rest of the weekend seemed to pass without event. By Sunday, Brittany joined in the meals, but she was the first to leave the table. Amber seemed to enjoy my quiet company when I was allowed to sit and eat. I can't say why, but it pleased me.

Monday found me a mess. I was ready for the cell phases quiz, but I was so upset over Brittany meeting with Chance after me, I could hardly concentrate on anything else. I felt like I was operating in the middle of dense fog. When I snapped back, I realized Chance was talking.

"So who do you believe is most at fault for the chain of events? Would the Prince be to blame, Friar Laurence, Friar John, Balthasar, either set of parents, the nurse, Benvolio, or someone else?"

"To blame?" I echoed.

Chance's intense blue eyes caught mine, and his hand dropped a little toward the table.

"Gigi, is... something wrong? You seem... distracted. Like you're preoccupied."

"It's nothing. I didn't sleep well last night, and I get more distracted when I'm tired."

"Okay. Well, you passed the cell phase quiz with flying colors. Great job."

"Really? I didn't miss any? I... was so nervous I thought I might have mixed up a couple of them."

"You passed it like a pro," Chance said. His dimples deepened as he looked at me.

My breath caught in my throat. Chance didn't seem aware of just how attractive he was. His eyes seemed perfectly spaced, not too wide or narrow. The vibrant color of them was one-of-a-kind. His nose was straight and seemed just the right size for his face. His lips were full and flanked by those dimples...

Just then, I realized I was staring.

Chance's expression held a question. I felt the hot flush charge up my cheeks, and I looked away.

"Um, I'm thirsty. Want some water?" I asked.

"Gigi, it's okay," Chance said gently. He reached out a hand, but I jumped up and retrieved two water bottles. When I sat back down, my face had cooled to some degree.

"So, uh, I think the Friar is the most responsible," I said.

"Friar Laurence or Friar John?"

"Laurence."

"Why?" His eyes searched my face. He seemed to be asking me personally rather than pertaining to the story.

"Because he's maintaining secrets. He accuses Romeo of being hot and cold with his love and warns him against a fast romance…. yet, turns around and marries them in hopes of ending the feud." I paused. "How can any marriage last if the courtship is one encounter?"

"Back then, marriages were arranged, without *any* encounters at times."

"Yes, but Friar Laurence is supposed to be a representative for morality and yet he lies. It was his idea to simulate Juliet's 'death' which was a catalyst for more events to go wrong. It's like he tries to help in all the wrong ways."

"So you believe a lie is not just words. It's actions."

"Most definitely. He deceived everyone except Romeo and Juliet, and he *instructed* them to lie."

Chance leaned as far back in the kitchen chair as it would permit. "And so you think that in the end, the friar's actions led to the tragedy."

"Of course. Yes, it was very tragic, but if you can set emotion aside, the friar's goal, ending the feud, *was* achieved. Just... at what cost?" My eyes met his.

"Yes, I suppose that's the truth of it, but so much tragedy could have been spared."

"Oh, I agree. But really, would it? Maybe Juliet would have killed herself sooner. Honesty would have been the best method. That and people acting like adults instead of children."

Chance laughed. I liked the sound of it.

"Very good. You're like a breath of fresh air."

"What do you mean?"

"Do you know how many students I've tutored on Shakespearean work? Many are very literal. I like how you think. It's... inspiring."

"Really?"

"Yes. But... I do have a question."

"What is it?"

"So, um, Juliet has no blame in the deception?"

I got the feeling we weren't just discussing the situation in *Romeo and Juliet.*

"Why yes, she has blame," I said, "but who could she trust, really? The nurse at first, but overall? Not really. And her parents?" I shook my head. "The people with power who control her destiny? I hate dishonesty, but you must agree, sometimes dishonesty is required."

We sat in silence for a few minutes. Before we were able to continue, the door to the mudroom off the garage opened. Brittany walked in, looking like she stepped out of a fashion magazine. Her hair was newly highlighted, and her makeup was perfectly applied. She held two upscale shopping bags in each hand, and I could see her freshly manicured nails gleaming. They were a faultless match to the shade of lipstick and the form-fitting red dress she wore.

"Oh, hello," she said, batting her eyes. "I'll be back. I'll just put up my stuff. See you in about fifteen, right?"

"Er, yes," Chance said.

Brittany exited with a pronounced swing of her hips.

I felt as if I were melting. My breathing increased, and my heart rate kicked up.

"Gigi?" Chance asked.

"Uh, yes?"

"You okay? You look a bit pale."

I made myself take a few breaths. "I get more anxiety when I'm tired," I said.

"You... were fine just a minute ago."

I knew Chance was pairing my anxiety with Brittany's appearance. I couldn't help my feelings, though.

"I'm okay."

"If you're sure?"

I nodded. "So, what do you want me to work on next time?"

"Remember, we have the literature test over parts of a plot and literary elements. Shakespeare will be on that as well. You really flew through that work."

I smiled. "Okay.   I could probably do that today.   I feel ready."

"There's not enough time.   I don't want you to feel rushed."

I uncapped my water and took a long drink. "Okay. What else?"

"See how many problems you can do, evens, and check your work in the back. Mark any you struggle with."

"Okay." I stood up.

"Hey, Gigi. We still have ten minutes."

How could I tell him that I wanted to be out of there when Brittany sashayed back in? She made me feel ill.

"We can't do much in that amount of time, can we?"

"No, but we can talk."

He pushed out my chair just a bit, so I sat.

"Is she mean to you?" he asked quietly.

I was taken aback. "Brittany?"

"Yes. Or any of them?"

"Brittany and I don't get along. Sometimes siblings are that way," I said with a shrug.

Chance didn't respond, but he looked at me. "You sure there's not more to it than that?"

Liz chose that moment to enter the kitchen. "You two about wrapped up?"

"Yes, ma'am," I said. "Chance gave me an outline for my next test. Now I just need to study and focus on some math homework."

"Don't forget your science and report in world cultures, as well."

"I won't. Thank you for all your help, Chance." I stood.

"Mrs. Chancellor, Gigi did very well on her quiz today. She made a hundred percent."

"That's good." Liz walked into the kitchen, took a cup out of the cabinet without looking at me and poured herself a glass of tea. "Would you like something to drink?" she asked. She leaned on the bar counter connecting the rooms.

"No, ma'am. Thank you."

I gathered up my books and was about to leave the room.

"Gigi." Liz looked directly at me for the first time since entering the room.

"Yes, ma'am?"

"It's your turn to cook dinner. Go put your stuff up and come on back to get it started."

Without meaning to, my shoulders slumped, and I had to quickly readjust all my books to keep them from toppling. Chance stood and helped me.

"Do you need help carrying them all?" he asked.

"Gigi can manage," Liz said. "She can make two trips if necessary."

"My, uh, room is where I keep them," I said.

"Yes, and we're proper in this house," Liz said.

The Collar Loosens

When I returned, Brittany was sitting in the chair next to Chance. She'd changed clothes and now wore a pink v-neck that clung to her curves and gave a peek at her cleavage. Her legs were crossed in fashionably faded jeans, and she wore socks instead of shoes.

An algebra book was opened in front of them. Brittany was looking up at Chance, leaning toward him. When she noticed me, she pointed to a problem in the book, shifting even closer. Chance pressed backwards into his chair, just a bit, to avoid contact.

He said, "I'd like to see you rework this problem for me. Write out every step so I can see your thought process."

"I hate writing each step down. It feels like I'm in high school again," Brittany complained with a silky smile and a bat of her eyes.

"You asked for help," Chance reminded her. He raised a dark brow. "This is how I can see how to help you."

"Oh, all right." Brittany bent over the paper and began writing. Chance and I made eye contact over her head. He smiled and my heart raced.

I bent over to get a pan.

"Seriously?" Brittany asked. She shot me a glare. "How am I supposed to concentrate with you cooking?"

"Mrs. Chancellor asked her to start dinner. Said it was her turn," Chance said.

"Oh, right," Brittany nodded, as if to herself, then gave me a smile. "Sorry, I forgot."

"I'll try to be quieter," I said.

I prepared some chicken for Alfredo. It was simple and easy. While the chicken cooked, I sliced up french bread. I knew Chance watched me because I felt his eyes on me from time to time.

I hated being in the kitchen during Brittany's session. She was a room away, but with the openness between the rooms, I could hear her coo. How could he resist her sultry voice? It was driving *me* crazy.

Just then, I heard Brittany ask, "Do you work out?"

I was sure my stepsister knew I couldn't resist looking. Right when my eyes touched on her, she smiled and put her hand on Chance's bicep.

"I, uh..." Chance said.

"I bet you do."

"Brittany, let's get back to this problem." Chance shifted in his chair and tapped the page.

"Okay. Just at least tell me what sports you play."

"I like soccer. I just play for fun, though."

"Ummm, you should invite me to a game."

"Well, that might be hard. I haven't played any real games since high school."

"Maybe you should think about it." Her voice was a low purr.

"Let's think about this math problem right now." Chance wrote down a problem and scooted the paper toward her.

She pouted and looked at him for a minute but leaned over and began to write.

Dinner was finally ready, and thankfully, Brittany's session drew to a close.

"So, um, if I have any questions about problems this week, can I text you?" Brittany asked. "I already have your number from that advertisement you posted."

"Uh, sure. Or you could just ask me a quick question after I work with Gigi."

"*Great.* Thanks." Brittany looked up at him through her long lashes, and a slow smile spread across her red lips.

"Will you want another session?" Chance asked, straightening.

"Yes, please. If you'd plan to see me regularly on Mondays, that would be perfect."

"Okay."

"And we can do a tutoring session, too," Brittany said with a giggle.

Chance gave what sounded like a forced laugh. I rolled my eyes. At least he didn't seem to be all into her. It made me happy.

After Chance left, I quickly set the table, and everyone was seated. I served then took my place.

"How did your session go?" Liz asked her daughter.

Brittany said, "It went great. I can see he's definitely interested in me, but he was shy in front of Gigi."

"He was?"

"Well, maybe distracted is a better word. She kept making noises while cooking."

"I see. Maybe I should have waited for her to cook."

"No, it's all good," Brittany smiled. "I don't want her thinking he's into her or anything. It's good for her to see that he's polite to everyone he works with."

Amber looked at me, and I just shrugged. I felt pretty happy. I was actually glad I'd been in the kitchen rather than not. At least I saw Chance's body language, and I didn't get the same reading that Brittany did.

Tuesday morning breakfast came and went. While I was cleaning up, the Chancellors remained at the kitchen table. Ethan looked over the paper while Liz held Ashton and kissed him. The toddler grunted and squirmed to escape.

"Sir? Ma'am?" I asked, waiting for their attention. Both looked at me.

"I - I was wondering... May I go for a walk... outside? Like around the block, or something?"

Ethan leaned back and looked thoughtful. He looked toward the brightly lit window.

"Absolutely not," Liz said as she put Ashton down.

"Actually, why not let her, Liz? It's not a bad idea," Ethan said. "See if Amber would like to accompany her?"

"She won't want to do that," Liz said. "She's got better things to do."

Ethan looked at me. "What brought this up?"

"Well, Sir, I grilled for you outside the other day, and it's not a secret I live here anymore. I just... would love to feel the sun on my skin. I never get to go outside. With tutoring, I realize that physical exercise is an important subject in school, and I just wanted to ask."

"You get plenty of exercise doing chores," Liz said.

"I see her point, though, Hon. Let's at least ask Amber. Maybe she would like that. What do you say?"

Liz's face hardened. Just then, Amber walked in the kitchen.

"Did someone say my name?" she asked. She looked back and forth to each of her parents.

"Liz?" Ethan asked again.

Liz's scowl did not change, but she gave a tiny nod.

"Yes, honey. Gigi would like to go for a walk. Would you want to walk with her? Perhaps around the block once or twice?"

"Oh, my God. You're actually going to let her get fresh air? I certainly would be *happy* to accompany her. Maybe we can get you an overdose of Vitamin D." Amber looked over at me. "Grab a jacket. Fall is in the wind."

"Okay."

I tried not to run back to my room, but *oh*, it was hard. I put on a hoodie and a jacket and tied my tennis shoes. Amber was dressed similarly when I reappeared.

"Come on, Gigi," Amber said with a smile.

She opened the door, and I was out in the bright sunshine. A cool breeze tugged on my hair. I closed my eyes and breathed in. I felt the radiance against my lids for just a moment.

Amber smiled at me and took my arm. "I'm proud of you," she whispered.

"For?"

"Finding the courage to ask," she said. "I'm glad they're finally starting to treat you better."

"Thanks to you, Amber. I truly am thankful. It's because of you."

"I think you're a very good person, Gigi. I'd like to get to know you better, if you'd like?"

I smiled in response. Amber did treat me the best of the Chancellors, but she had been in my life for eight years, and she was just now starting to stand up for me. *Could I really trust her? She'd been a child herself for most of those years,* I reminded myself. That *was* a pretty good excuse. Children couldn't stand up to authority figures, not really.

We began to walk. I shivered just a bit when the wind picked up.

"Are you cold?" Amber asked.

"Not really. I'm just not used to feeling cool air blow against my skin."

"I know," Amber said. "I feel really bad about that."

We walked for a bit in silence.

"We could do this at least three or four times a week, if you want."

"Really?" I felt tears pool in the corners of my eyes. Gratitude welled in my breast. "Thank you, Amber. Thank you for your kindness."

"You're welcome, Gigi. You deserve it."

She leaned toward me and gave me a quick hug.

The next three weeks passed fairly uneventfully. Amber and I enjoyed nice walks, and Chance and I made great progress.   It still upset me to see how Brittany acted around the handsome tutor, but I was happy to see that Chance kept it strictly business.

Slip of the Tongue

Friday afternoon, I heard a knock at the front door, and I walked quickly to open it.

"Good afternoon," the familiar tenor said.

"Good afternoon." I smiled happily.

Chance came in and was silhouetted against the brilliant backdrop for a moment.

"It's a beautiful day out there. Won't have too many more of them before it's bonfire weather."

"That sounds fun."

"Bonfires?"

"Yes."

Chance glanced around the house. "I suppose there's an ordinance in this neighborhood against them."

I shrugged. I really didn't know if there was or not, but I just knew that wasn't something the Chancellors engaged in.

"Do you go to a lot of bonfires?" I asked.

He nodded.

"Tell me what they're like."

Royal blue eyes met mine. "You've never been to one?"

I looked down and shook my head.

Liz poked her head from the dining room. "Oh, you're still by the door? You don't need to be wasting valuable time chit-chatting. Sit at the table and get to work. This is my dime you're on."

"Yes, ma'am," I said.

Chance lifted his brows and mouthed, "O-kay."

Although irritated, I had to swallow a giggle.   Even Chance's reactions were attractive.

We moved to the table. Liz walked to the coffee pot and poured herself a cup.

"Does your family have any plans over the weekend, Mrs. Chancellor?" Chance asked when she leaned on the arched doorway between the rooms. "It's going to be lovely weather."

"Not big ones," she said, raising the coffee to her lips. "I want to take Ashton to a corn maze and maybe let him have some fun painting a pumpkin.

"That does sound like fun. It's almost time for Trick-or-Treating."

Liz nodded with a smile before her glance flicked to me. I opened up my math.

"Can you help me understand this word problem?"

Chance leaned over to read it. "Of course. First you want to assign a value to every item mentioned. Then you can see what information the question calls for versus the excess data."

We spent nearly an hour on math. In between subjects, we usually took a small break. I got up to get two bottles of water. I glanced around to make sure Liz wasn't nearby.

"Can I ask you something?" I whispered when I sat back down.

"You can ask me anything."

"How old are you?"

"Well, that wasn't what I was expecting." He smiled.

"What were you expecting?" I inquired.

"Oh, I don't know. Something more... mysterious. Like to give me a hint about what these people are really like."

"Oh, no," I laughed. "Just your age."

"I'm barely twenty. I'm in my junior year in college, thanks to my high school for offering dual enrollment with college classes."

"So, you're only about two years older than me."

Chance nodded. Then, he quickly looked down at me.

"You're eighteen? I felt like that was so, but Mrs. Chancellor led me to believe you were younger."

"Oh, God."

"What, Gigi?"

"Oh, God, Oh, God, *Oh, God!*"

"Gigi, *talk* to me."

"Chance, you can't tell anyone. I slipped about my age."

"What are you talking about?" Chance asked, straightening.

My breathing rate was increasing. "I - I forgot. Liz told Mr. Ponder I was fifteen... uh, to help explain how far behind I was in my education. She also told him I have a learning disability."

"You most certainly don't act like you have a disability... in my opinion," Chance said.

"Chance, please, *please* don't let on to *anyone* you know my true age. Please."

Chance held up his hands. "Okay, Gigi. If it's that important to you, I won't."

"It is. More important than you can realize."

Chance stared at me for a few moments. His gaze was intense, and I shrunk down in my chair.

"Gigi, look. I want to help you. I wish you trusted me enough to give me more than tiny insights. Please."

"Chance, you're my friend, but I just can't. Not yet." *Not ever.* "I'm sorry."

Unintentionally, I leaned toward him. I could feel his warmth envelop me although we were barely touching. A tear trickled down my cheek, and he swiped a tissue from the counter and handed it to me. I quickly wiped away the betrayal just as Liz walked back into the room.

I jumped a little while Liz poured herself another cup of coffee and stared at us.

"You making progress?"

"Yes, ma'am," Chance said. "I'm giving Gigi a moment to prepare. I had her do research and a report, and she's organizing her thoughts before giving a demonstration. Presentation is the first step toward adult responsibilities."

"Hum."

"It will help her to be more prepared for one-on-one interviews, like for future jobs. It's a good first step to overcoming anxiety in similar situations."

Liz gave a nod and left the room. I took a deep breath.

I whispered, "Thanks, Chance."

After another moment or two, I gave my spiel on Japanese culture and customs.

Near the end of our session, Chance touched my arm. "You okay?"

"Only if you hold to your promise."

"I give you my word. I don't want you to have anxiety over a silly slip."

"Thank you, Chance."

He nodded then stood. "I'll see you on Monday."

When Chance left, Liz was really worked up. She turned around and smacked me across the face.

"You little floozy! Flirting with him like that!"

"Ma'am?" I asked. My hand clutched the site of my throbbing cheek. Tears burned in my eyes that I dared not let fall.

"Don't act like you don't know what I'm talking about," she hissed.

I knew better than to disagree with Liz. I wasn't flirting. I'd been pleading with Chance to keep my secret.

The next few days were excruciating. Liz had me doing every dirty chore she could think of. Scrubbing out the toilets by hand was especially detestable. She relented enough to give me time to do my homework, but it was very difficult for me to think because I was so tired.

"We're going to have to get you a warmer coat," Amber said.

I just nodded.

We were halfway through our exercise routine on Sunday afternoon. We were up to a mile and a half.

"Gigi..."

I looked up.

"I'm going to try to help you more. I see that bruise on your face. Did Mom do that?"

I nodded again.

"Why?"

"She thought I was flirting with Chance."

"Who *wouldn't* flirt with him?" She smiled, but it quickly died on her lips.

"But I didn't."

She lightly touched my arm. "I believe you. Look, I didn't mean to downplay what happened. Mom's a nut. I'm so sorry. I'll try to have a talk with her. This *has* to stop."

I was nervous to meet with Chance because of the way Liz was treating me but regardless, Monday still arrived.

When those brilliant baby blues settled on me from across the table, I noticed his intense stare.

"Wh – what?" I asked.

"How did you get that bruise?" he finally asked in a lowered voice.

"Uh, I have a bruise?"

Chance cocked a brow. He wasn't buying it. He sat and waited for a different response.

"I fell when I got up at night to go to the bathroom. I really need to replace the night light bulbs..." I mumbled. Then I shrugged.

"I notice you're sitting further away from me, too." He paused. "Why do you protect these people, Gigi? I'm sure I can get you somewhere safe."

I shook my head and looked down. How could I tell him about the continued threats on my real family? My life had been sacrificed for them because I loved them. It wasn't their fault I'd been snatched away; that was on me.

I'd been innocent and Sally and Nick had prayed on my naiveté, but that didn't change the fact that I'd disobeyed my father. My wonderful father... my lovely mother... my cherished baby brother. What I wouldn't do to see them again.

"Gigi?" an intriguing voice sailed to me from somewhere.

Suddenly, I ripped myself out of my reveries. I needed to stop thinking about my missed family. I'd given up on seeing them again until much later in life. Someday, yes, I would. They couldn't hold me captive forever... *could they?*

Chance's hand reached out across the table and found mine. My fingers curled softly into his before I tried to focus on the use of time.

"Gigi, talk to me. Please let me help you."

All I could do for that moment was look into his royal blue eyes.

"Chance, uh, what do you want to concentrate on first?"

Chance kept looking at me intensely for a good measure of time before finally, he sighed and pulled out the biology book.

Although I cared deeply for Chance, I couldn't confide my life story. It was nice to feel closer to him than I had anyone since Lucinda.

"Gigi, I'm sure you don't get to have a phone, but if you ever need me and want to call, here's my number."

Chance slid a phone number scribbled on the back of a piece of paper. I slid it in my pocket, next to Mr. Ponder's business card. I was glad that I had both of these caring men's contact information. I doubted I'd ever get the courage to make that call, but it was reassuring to have. It comforted me to know a small connection to them was next to me at all times.

I settled back and turned to the biome chapter. We worked for about an hour. About this time, Liz stepped in the kitchen and put on a pot of coffee. I was sure it was just to have a reason to pass through the dining room frequently without looking suspicious.

After pouring a cup, Liz turned to Chance. "Do you mind working with Brittany a little longer today? She has a big test coming up, and she'd like extra help."

"Um, sure, Mrs. Chancellor. I'm glad to help."

When Liz left the room, I'm sure I looked crestfallen.

"Gigi, what's the matter?" Chance finally asked.

"Nothing," I grumbled.

He flashed a dazzling smile. "I think I might know," he confided.

"Oh yeah?" I asked.

His eyes were twinkling at me. A ghost of a slow, sexy smile twitched his lips. "So... you have nothing to be jealous of."

"Jealous?" I whisper vehemently. "Who says I'm jealous?"

"Maybe I'm just hoping you are."

I didn't know what to say to that. My typical response to embarrassment was to look down. Even through my curtain of hair, I felt Chance's eyes on me. Still, I could not wipe the happy grin from my face.

"Gigi, just for the record, I'm just appeasing your... *mom.*"

I sighed then frowned as I looked up.

"I have no interest in Brittany personally. It's just money to me."

"You don't know how they work."

"No, you're right. I don't. Wanna tell me about it?" he asked hopefully.

"If you play with fire, you're going to get burned is what I've always heard," I said.

"If you won't tell me more, I'll just have to find out the hard way," Chance warned. He cocked his head at me.

"They just manage to take every good thing away from me." The words slipped before I could take them back.

"Now we're getting somewhere," he said.

I turned my attention to my paper. I didn't say anything for a few moments. When I found my voice, I said, "Um, can you show me again how to solve quadratic equations?"

Fundraiser for Project Graduation

I felt happier than I had in a long time. Chance revealed a tiny spark of interest in me. I could *feel* it. Not only that, but I also had the phone numbers in my pocket. While I endured Liz screaming at me and calling me many names, I would reach down and touch the pocket. It was like a part of my friends were with me, and I didn't feel as isolated.

Several days later, Amber came home excited. Brittany and Liz were standing at the counter in the kitchen discussing what I should prepare for the evening meal.

"Mom?" Amber said slightly out of breath.

"Yes?"

"Guess what? We have a big dance coming up!" Amber plopped down on a bar stool.

"Oh, yay!" Liz breathed. She loved indulging her daughters as much as they enjoyed being pampered.

"Is this dance for a special occasion?" I asked.

Brittany glared at me as if I hadn't spoken.

"Yes," Amber answered, nodding at me. She turned back to Liz, "Mom, we all voted on it as a class. We're putting this dance on for Project Graduation. All money raised will go towards paying for our activities after graduation."

"Isn't that where they have a lock-in party to keep kids from getting drunk after they graduate from high school?" Liz asked.

"Yes. It saves lives. And this dance will be for *all* high school families. They can even bring outsiders as dates so we can get a lot of entrance fees. We're holding it downtown at the old castle. So it's a school function but really, it's not."

Liz squealed and did a happy dance while swinging Amber around in a circle.

"And guess what, Mom?" Amber waited only a moment. "The theme is Orlana, so we can wear pretty gowns."

I dropped my scrub brush. No one noticed my reaction.

Amber said, "Brittany, you can go, too."

Brittany grinned slowly, and her eyes slid over to me for a second. "Mom, that's awesome! Um... do you think that maybe... Chance would want to go with me?"

"I don't know, honey. He's probably a little past high school dances."

"So am I, but it's for a good cause. I'm going to ask him anyway. We're basically the same age except he took college classes in high school."

"Suit yourself."

I couldn't take any more and ran from the room while silent tears scorched my cheeks. Everything I'd ever loved was taken away by these people. Because of them, my first idol, Orlana, was magical no more. My beloved childhood romance was marred forever by that fateful day, but still, the enchantment couldn't be entirely erased.   A sliver of a charmed memory was entwined with the tale: the love that my parents had shown by making my dreams come true.   In my heart, there would always be a memorable flare when the word 'Orlana' was mentioned.

However, at that moment, the pain associated with that character burned more brightly.   The thought of Brittany asking Chance to go to the dance with her was more than I could bear.   For the first time in a very long time, I could not turn off the tears, and I fled for my room.

Shortly after, Liz's shadow filled my doorway.   I could feel her satisfaction at my misery, but for once, she said nothing.   She withdrew and left me to my sorrow.

The next day found me in a similar state: I was filled with sadness.   Most of the time, I was able to push down my own feelings of loss and despair, but now that it had raised its ugly head, it was not going to give up the fight easily.

Liz gave me slightly less chores, but I knew she expected a deeper clean than normal.   At least when I was scrubbing, my thoughts weren't as focused on the horrors of my life.

"After supper is cleaned up," Liz instructed.   "I want you to do some of your homework. You'll have to skip your walk today. Chance will be here tomorrow, and I don't think you've done much."

I didn't respond.

"Gigi!   Acknowledge me when I'm talking to you."

"Yes, ma'am."

<><><>

When Chance arrived, I couldn't bear to look at him directly. His brilliant eyes studied me as I made a show of gathering my school materials. Right when we sat down to work, Chance reached out and touched my arm. Silently, his eyes questioned me, but I avoided direct contact.

"Gigi, talk to me," he whispered. "What's wrong?"

"PMS," I stated. "Sometimes we women just feel sad. Please bear with me, and I'm sorry if this is too much personal information."

"I – I, uh, understand," he stuttered.

I could tell he was torn on whether to believe me or to wonder further. His eyes explored what he could see of my body and skin. I knew he was looking for another tell-tale sign of abuse, but I was certain the blood oozing from my heart-felt stabs couldn't be detected.

"Gigi..."

"Yes?"

"Um, would you... be okay if I asked for permission for you to go out with me?"

"What?" I asked, dropping my pencil. I couldn't believe my ears.

"Um, would you agree to go out with me if I asked Liz?"

"Oh, Chance!" I whispered.   My heart was suddenly singing.   A tremulous smile graced my lips, and I felt nearly dizzy with the rush of blood to my face.   "B – but you can't."

"What?   Why not?"

"She would never agree."

"Does she let Brittany date?"

"She's older than me."

"Well, is the younger girl allowed to date?"

"Girl?   Do you mean Amber?

Chance chuckled.   "I was referring to gender, not age.   Is the young *woman*, uh, Amber, allowed to date?"

"I – I – , um, yes, of course. I'm sure she's going to the dance," I paused. "She's very excited about it. We're the same age, but remember, Liz is pretending I'm fifteen."

"Damn," Chance murmured. Then he looked up. "What dance?"

"The dance Brittany is going to ask you to," I blurted out.

Chance's handsome brows shot up in surprise.   "*She's* going to ask *me* out?"

"Yes.   And I, uh, know Liz will kill me if you want to go out with me instead."

"Doesn't a man get a say on who he sees around here?" he asked.

I didn't answer and just looked down.   Suddenly, his larger hand covered mine in a slight but firm grip.   The comforting heat radiated into my colder one.

"She'll have to let you out," he said in a conspirator's voice.

"How so?"

"She's not fond of DFS investigations. I can remind her that even adopted kids should have the right to be normal, especially if it's something that her other children are allowed to do."

I nodded glumly.

"Don't fret. We'll work it out."

"Well, she still won't let me go with you. Remember, you're technically an adult where I'm *fifteen*."

Chance's confidence gave me hope. Even if I wasn't able to go with him, I was joyful for his interest. I really didn't know what he saw in me, but I wasn't going to look a gift horse in the mouth.

When it was Brittany's turn to work with the striking man, I knew I'd better disappear. Typically, when Chance was here, I went to my room to work on homework. It couldn't be my turn to cook every Friday, and it would never do for him to see me slaving away.

A few days later, the doorbell rang. Liz was home with Ashton while I was cleaning the baseboards.

"Get to your room. If it's that prick from DFS, get clean clothes on, pronto. Tell him you were doing homework."

"Yes, ma'am."

I charged quietly down the hall while Liz answered the summons.

"Well hello, Mr. Ponder," Liz greeted quite loudly.

On cue, I donned clean clothes and went back to the living room.

"Hello, Mrs. Chancellor, Gigi."

He received a cool nod from Liz and a happy smile from me.

"To what do we owe this pleasant surprise?" Liz asked sweetly.

"I just wanted to check in on Gigi and her progress," he said. "In fact, with your permission, I'd like you to call Chance and see if he's available. That way we can talk as a group and there's no miscommunication."

"Fine. I wasn't planning on a meeting today, though. It would have been nice... no, *considerate*," Liz paused, "if you'd have let us know in advance."

"Well, if you weren't home, I'd just have come back at a later time. We do like the element of our visits being unplanned in many instances. Please, call your tutor in."

Forty-five minutes later, Chance was led into the living room.

"Hello, young man," Mr. Ponder greeted.

"Hello, Mr. Ponder."

"Sorry to disrupt your day, but I just wanted to have a brief meeting. If we're all here, it's less likely for miscommunication to occur."

"I understand."

"We're here to discuss Gigi." He looked at me. "How do you feel your instruction is going, young lady?

What would you like to see improved? Do you get enough study time?”

“Sir, my mom couldn’t have picked a better tutor. I have learned so much from Chance. I can’t say that there’s anything I would improve. And, uh, I have enough time to complete all my work.”

“Chance?”

“Mr. Ponder, Liz is aware, as well as Gigi, her progress has been phenomenal. Her reading has jumped up four grade levels. I’d say her reading is at an eighth grade level right now, but by the end of the year, I guarantee, she’ll be at grade level.”

“Sophomore?” Liz asked.

I answered before Chance could. “I plan to be at a senior level reading,” I said. “I’m not stopping at a sophomore level.”

I angled my body so I was unable to see any glare from Liz.

“That’s a lofty goal, and at this rate, I’m sure you’ll achieve it,” Mr. Ponder said. He turned to Chance. “That says a lot about your teaching style. Maybe you should reconsider your future career goal.”

“Thank you, sir. I may just do that.” He shrugged. “I’m still undecided.”

“Very good. What about other areas?”

“Math is progressing well. All subjects are, really. Math builds, as you know, so I’d say that and science are a little behind history and English. Typical. We all have subjects we enjoy more than others.”

“What grade level would you say she is?”

"I'd call her math probably pre-algebra level, but she does understand some concepts in geometry. Overall, though, pre-algebra."

I nodded in agreement.

"Simply amazing."

Liz nodded with a smile.

"The biggest area Gigi needs to work on now is presentation. Talking in front of people she doesn't know very well. Good news, though. I hear all the girls have an outing planned soon. It's a great way to progress her socialization," Chance added with a hint of a smile. "It'll be a great ice breaker."

Liz and I stared at him.

"Brittany tells me the girls are attending a dance to raise money for Project Graduation."

"Oh, how nice," Mr. Ponder said. "Gigi, do you feel ready for such an entrance into society?"

"I - I, um..."

Liz leaned forward. "I, ah, don't think she's quite ready for that step."

"Nonsense," Mr. Ponder said.

"Brittany asked me to go," Chance said. "I'd love to go with all three young ladies. I think it would help Gigi feel more at ease. Then she'd have her two sisters and me to make her feel more comfortable."

"All..." Liz looked momentarily confused, "THREE?" she asked, shooting to her feet. Gone was her smile. Now her lips were a slash of white on her face. An awkward silence stretched while Liz struggled for composure.

"Yes, ma'am.   What a novel idea. All three," Mr. Ponder confirmed. "It would help Gigi's anxiety if she is supported. It makes perfect sense."

"In my day, a man only took one girl to a dance," Liz finally managed. "And I know Brittany wanted to go with him... just him and not her... sisters." Her eyes slid sideways toward me before she forced them back to the man in the chair.

Chance said, "I insist. I think taking all three of your daughters, if they're willing, is perfect for introducing Gigi back into society. People with anxiety need lots of support. There's no better network than family."

Mr. Ponder nodded. "I agree: it would be a wonderful introduction into social settings for Gigi."

"Gigi *cannot* go!   She's too nervous in large group settings."

Mr. Ponder said, "I'm afraid she's going to have to overcome her fear. That's one step she's missing from a school setting. Presentation. This would be the lowest level. She'll need to have a job someday. So why not start now?"

"What is the meaning of this?   How dare you come into my house and tell me how to treat my own children!"

"Actually, I'm not telling you how to treat your own children. I'm *suggesting* to you that you treat your adopted child the same as you do your biological children."

"Of all the nerve!" Liz hissed. "You're insisting that my other children are punished... by not allowing them to take dates."

Mr. Ponder smiled. "I am not suggesting that at all. You could ask your daughters to go with Gigi without Chance. One could keep her company while the other dances with her date."

"And if we refuse?"

"That is the question," Mr. Ponder replied vaguely. He shrugged his shoulders noncommittally.

"What does that mean?" Liz asked.

"What do you think it means?" Mr. Ponder reflected.

"OOOHHH, you are *impossible*!" Liz walked to the enormous fireplace and back.

The older man nodded once in agreement. He shifted toward Chance. "So if you were to take the three Chancellor girls to the dance, how would that work?"

"Well, Gigi and her sisters would go with me to the dance. The sisters would help Gigi feel comfortable and introduce her to their friends. Then, I suppose, I could dance a dance with each of them if they choose."

"Um, I don't think I'm ready to do any dancing," I offered.

Liz glared at me. "This is ridiculously impossible! Brittany will never agree to this!"

"She doesn't have to agree," Mr. Ponder said.

"She doesn't?" Liz asked hopefully.

"I suppose we could try to get her paired with a Big Sister. I can request an accelerated match. That means regular outings between the two once they're paired. I'd have to make arrangements with you so that Gigi could meet her match ahead of this dance and develop a bit of rapport. That way, she'll have someone to talk to anyway. If your daughters aren't willing to support their sister. Or even if they insist on spending the entire night with their dates."

Liz began wearing a path on the floor. I could feel the anger radiating off her. I was sure I'd be in for a terrible tongue lashing and chore list once Mr. Ponder left. Finally, she stopped.

"What if Brittany asks a friend to take Gigi. Would that work?"

"I'm afraid not. Gigi has a relationship built on trust with Chance and, uh, your daughters. She would have even more anxiety if she were to go with a person she didn't know, especially if it were perceived to be a date. She isn't ready for that. Gigi needs this outing into the world, and it's best if she's supported by people who care about her."

A small, exasperated sound strangled in Liz's throat.

"Mama?" Ashton asked, toddling up to her. She swung her four-year-old into her arms and tried to mask her shaking.

"I'll take my leave now, but as a last word of advice, I sincerely hope all three girls' dresses will be of similar value. Good day." Mr. Ponder winked at me as he took his leave. "Let me know what you decide about the Big Sisters Program. It would be a great intervention to implement with Gigi, even excluding the dance."

"Wait, Mr. Ponder. I'll walk out with you." Chance stood to leave.

As soon as the door shut, I ran to my room to put my work clothes back on. When I heard Liz's enraged scream, I began to shake. I immediately went to work as far away from her as I could.

My New Friend

I knew the evening meal would be a strained affair, so I took the extra time to create an extravagant meal to hopefully ease some of the tension.

Liz's fury radiated out in a nearly tangible wave. When everyone sat, Ethan looked at his wife, but she ignored him and continued to stare at me.

I poured the turkey and wild rice soup appetizer into bowls and placed them beside their salad bowls. While they worked on the dishes, I arranged the pork loin and red skin potato mash onto china platters and sat them on the table as the entree. I topped their tea glasses before sitting.

When my first bite was halfway to my mouth, Liz spoke up.

"Gigi has some interesting news to share."

Everyone except Ashton stopped eating momentarily.

I lowered my spoon. With a look at Liz, I said, "Um, Mr. Ponder visited and asked Chance to come to a brief meeting about my progress?"

Ethan said, "*Really?* That's pretty presumptuous. So Ponder came over, unannounced, I'll guess, and demanded a meeting?"

"Yes," Liz confirmed. "And?"

I cleared my throat. "I've made very good progress in my tutoring. I'm about four grade levels from where I should be."

"As a senior or as a sophomore?" Brittany sneered.

Amber smiled at me. "Just ignore her, Gigi. I think that's great. Good job."

Liz's stony expression didn't soften. "Tell about his demands." Her eyes hadn't flickered in their perusal of me.

"Like what?" Ethan asked.

"What's the news that *you know* I want you to share?" Liz asked, narrowing eyes.

"Gigi? Care to explain further?" Ethan's gaze shifted from his wife back to me.

I swallowed. "Um, Chance brought up the dance. He told Mr. Ponder that all the Chancellor girls were going. Mr. Ponder assumed that included me."

Ethan's mouth gaped open, and he looked at Liz. "You mean you're going to let her go to the dance?"

"I don't know what to do, Ethan. Do you have any suggestions?"

"Can you request to be a chaperone?"

"No, Mom. You can't be a chaperone," Brittany interrupted. "I'm going with Chance, and I plan to have fun."

"It will be chaperoned, Brittany," Liz said. "But I have no intention of going. You and Amber will have to keep an eye on Gigi."

"I'll be busy," Brittany said. She wiggled into her chair with a superior smile glued to her face.

"Um, Chance offered to escort all of you. *Including* Gigi. To make her first appearance more... comfortable for her. He insisted. Ponder liked the idea. Chance wouldn't be her date, just so you know. It's merely to ease her into public."

"Mom! No!" Brittany said. She slammed down her cup.

"I think it's a great idea," Amber said. She looked at me and smiled before shifting her attention back to her mother. "I think you all are doing great letting up on her, but she still needs more... exposure to social situations. Personally, I'd love to go with her!"

Liz said, "Then Amber, it'll be mainly your job to keep an eye on her." She looked at her oldest daughter and said, "I have no choice, dear. Believe me, I probably like this less than you do."

"I doubt that," Brittany said, "I refuse to share my date with *her*."

Brittany scooted back from the table and left the room. Her angry footsteps echoed down the hall.

About ten o'clock that evening, I heard stomping coming down the stairs. I was working on a writing assignment in my room. The marching feet were headed in my direction. The door flung open, and Brittany stood in the entryway. Her hands were clenched into fists, and her face was flushed.

"You little bitch! How dare you tread on my property!"

I didn't respond. I knew she'd marked Chance as hers, and I was going to get the blame for her not getting her way.

"Don't you have anything to say for yourself?" she screeched.

"Brittany, believe it or not, I don't want to go to this dance. I don't seem to have a choice."

"Yeah, right!" she said, throwing a cup at me. "You KNOW I asked him to go with me!"

"This wasn't my idea," I repeated, holding my hands up.

"You're truly a bitch!" she screamed. Then she spun on her heels and left.

<><><>

"So how have things been?" Chance asked me at the next available opportunity.

"Horrible and wonderful."

His grin told me he knew exactly what I meant.

"But they haven't..."

"Beat me? No. I've had more chores on my list, though." I forced a laugh.

"How did Brittany take it?"

"Not well. She won't be here for her tutoring session, by the way."

"Okay. I'm not surprised, honestly."

"Me, either."

"I wonder when Liz is going to tell me."

"Probably as soon as my time is up."

"Yes. In other words, 'Get the hell out!'"

We had difficulty suppressing our laughter.

"Chance?"

"Yes?"

"Honestly, I truly am going to be nervous getting out in public. I don't know how to dance."

"You'll be the life of the party, Gigi."

I looked down. "I doubt that."

214

"Hey," he said, gently cupping my chin and lifting my head up until I met his eyes. "I'll be there to help."

While I smiled, his response was dazzling.

"Now I have a question for you," he said.

"What?"

"If you could have any name in the world on this magical night, what would you want me to call you?"

"Orlana?"

"You got it."

"On second thought, I've always loved the name 'Zoey'."

"Well, I'm going to call you Zoey on our outing."

Outing? I loved the sound of that.

"Just please don't call me that around my... family. They can't stand the thought that I might have fun."

"You got it."

<><><>

The next few weeks were miserable for me. The family ignored my existence unless it was to bark another command in my direction. I shook my head. *That's not entirely true.* Mostly, it was Liz and Brittany. Ethan was neutral, and Ashton was too little. Amber tried to stick up for me, wonderfully, and we continued our walking schedule.

<><><>

One evening, Amber loaned me a coat of hers until I could get one of my own. It was a little later than our usual stroll.

"Gigi, I'm sorry Mom and Brittany are being so mean to you. It's not your fault that Mr. Ponder insists that you go. I think it's actually a good idea to have Chance and me go to support you. Just so you know, I don't have a choice. Mom's making me keep an eye on you," she said. "I'm sure if I didn't agree to be your two-on-one date, she would refuse to let you go even with Mr. Ponder's, um, *suggestion*."

"I know," I responded then blushed. "Um, I don't know if I'd call it a date," I giggled.

"I'm sure you do know, and yes," she laughed, "I'm calling it a date. At first, I was kinda mad that I can't get a date of my own, but spoiled Brittany always gets her way."

"Well, not... *always*," I said with a tiny smile.

Amber snorted then laughed. "You're right. This one time, you got the prize, and she's pissed! She's a poor sport. My sister doesn't know how to handle losing."

"I can tell. She threw a cup at me last night."

"Really?"

"Yes. About ten o'clock. She stomped in my room, called me a bitch several times, and threw a cup at me."

Amber giggled. "I'm sorry, but I've been on the receiving end many times. I would have loved to see your face."

"I was a bit surprised. At least the cup didn't get me."

"No, her aim is bad."
"Thank goodness."
We both laughed.

The date of the dance was rapidly approaching. My studies were also going well, but the closer to the outing, the more nervous I became. It was getting harder to focus, and I think Chance noticed.

"Relax," my tutor advised. "Take a few deep breaths when you start to feel anxious. This first step will be the hardest."

"Chance, I can't even think."

"The only thing we have to fear is fear itself," he quoted.

No, not really, I thought. I was nervous about being in a crowded event, but I was slightly more worried about how the adults in this house would treat me upon my return. That was scary, petrifying, and I'd rather not even go than to face that music.

"Hey," Chance said softly, grabbing my hands. "We're going to have a good time!"

"I know. Believe it or not, I really am looking forward to it."

"Then just relax," he encouraged. "We've gotta get through the next few chapters today before we can stop."

"I know," I said miserably. My mind was just not on my studies.

<><><>

It was early, and breakfast was already steaming. I had mounds of scrambled eggs, piles of golden toast settled close by with creamy soft butter in a crystal container, crisp and chewy bacon, and velvety oatmeal sweetened with brown sugar and cinnamon. All the dishes were arranged expertly on the table. I'd even made a few pancakes to be adorned by rich maple syrup so that everyone would be satisfied.

Ethan and Liz came down the stairs. A sleepy-eyed boy squirmed in his father's arms. When they'd settled into their seats, I poured Ethan coffee and Liz a glass of frothy orange juice. Then I hurried up the stairs to wake the girls. For once, Brittany wasn't as difficult to wake up.

"I suppose you're in such a good mood because we have to take you shopping today," she grumbled.

I didn't say anything, but mentally nodded. Then I left to wake up her sister.

"Good morning, Amber," I sang.

She rolled over and groaned.

"It's time to rise and shine!"

She cracked an eye and peered at me.

"I made you pancakes," I bribed conspiratorially.

"Thanks," she said. She offered a sleepy smile.

"You're welcome. See you downstairs!"

"Hey," she called.

"Yes?" I said, turning back.

"I'm glad you get to go shopping with us. I'll be discreet, but I'll make sure mom gets you a nice dress."

"Aww," I managed. "Th – thank you, Amber."

She smiled then rolled over for a few more minutes.

I never realized that Amber wasn't truly one of them, but when I stopped to actually think about it, she had never been mean to me. She always treated me with quiet dignity. It was an epic moment to feel a connection with someone in this family.

After I served the household breakfast, ate, and scoured the kitchen, I ran to my room to put on my nicest things. I wore a pair of fitted jeans, a fashion tee, and donned my light-weight jacket. I was an excited mess.

Liz was not happy to have to take me, so she and Brittany didn't acknowledge my presence, but Amber was satisfied to sit in the back seat with me as we traveled to a bridal store for our first stop in our quest for the perfect Orlana dress.

Right away, Brittany squealed in delight and headed for the most expensive rack. I was overwhelmed immediately. A sales lady approached, but Amber waved her toward her sister and mother.

"Come on," she said. "We'll look over here. We're about the same size except you may have a little more upstairs."

I know my eyes widened with surprise. I'd never really thought about my physique. For most of my life, I'd worn hand-me-down ill-fitting clothes, and I worked non-stop. It's only been in the past year that my clothes fit more true to my size, but I'd never had a moment to consider my appearance. I blushed with embarrassment.

Amber snickered good-naturedly.

"Come on," she said again and pulled me in the direction of vibrantly colored dresses.

I mostly stood in a daze. I was a robot, holding the dresses that Amber piled in my arms. Mechanically, I shuffled toward the dressing room with Amber chatting in my ear. I'd never touched such delicate creations, and now I was saturated with them.

Finally, I was able to mutter, "Are you sure we won't be... overdressed?"

"Oh, just go with it! Yes, of course, we'll be overdressed! This isn't prom, but what better excuse to dress up than going to a princess dance?"

I didn't know what to say, so I just stood there while she piled the dresses in the fitting room.

"You go first."

"Wh – what do you mean?" I gasped.

"I mean you are going to try on the dresses first until the *one* speaks to us."

"B – but..."

"No buts."

"But... your, um, mom."

"I said no buts!" She giggled to soften my fear. "Look, I'll take care of her."

The next thirty minutes I tried on several dresses. Finally, I came out in a pale pink design. The skirt flared out delicately from the fitted waist, and the hemline did remind me somewhat of a faery creation. A white ribbon at the waist, encrusted with brilliance, pieced the top of the dress to the bottom. The front of the bodice was heart-shaped, also lined in crystals, and modestly suggested the fullness housed beneath. When I stepped into the illumination positioned over the mirrors, the light caught on the fabric and exploded into dazzling shimmers that turned the light shade of pink into an iridescent rainbow.

"Oh, my God, Gigi! That dress was made for you!" Amber breathed. "The color of the fabric fits your skin perfectly!"

The glamour of the formality took my breath away. It was way too fine for the likes of me.

"Oh, no... I couldn't! I mean, it was fun trying it on and all..."

"Oh, yes, you will! I insist! I have quite a bit of allowance. This dress is yours!" she cried. "No matter what mom says," she added in a low voice.

I couldn't speak. I replaced the finery with my items from the second-hand store. I sat in numbed silence and nodded approval at all the beautiful gowns Amber tried on. Finally, my friend settled on a molten-gold dress. Rich fabric layers cascaded over a sheath, and a million diamonds twinkled from the folds. It truly encased the wearer in finery suitable for a princess.

I barely paid attention when Amber also fitted both of us with matching jewelry and shoes. Finally, we saw the sales lady leading the other two family members to the purchase counter. A lively blood-red dress was encased in a protective bag. Gold piping snaked throughout the form-fitting ensemble.

"Did you find anything, Amber?" Liz asked happily.

"Yes, Mom. Both Gigi and I are ready to check out."

"I hope you looked on the clearance rack for…" she cleared her throat then continued, "Gigi."

"Nope," Amber responded cheerfully.

Liz stiffened. I could tell she really wanted to make a scene but thought better of it.

Amber lowered her voice. "Mom, you've got to be careful. With you-know-who snooping around, you don't want to take a chance with buying less for Gigi. Roll with the punches. I'm thinking of what's best for all of us."

Liz's face relaxed and she managed a tight-lipped smile. "Of course, you're right, dear. Thank you for reminding me."

Brittany's endless chatter about her dress and how beautiful she'd be filled the otherwise silent car. I was relieved I didn't have to speak about the astronomical purchases made on my behalf. I was still in awe.

Reliving a Nightmare

Finally, it was the day before the dance. I was on pins and needles when Chance appeared for our normal tutoring lessons. I was so beside myself, there was no way I could concentrate.

I sat down next to the handsome tutor and shifted in my seat. I picked up my pencil and put it down. I fiddled with anything that wasn't attached to the table.

"Hey," Chance began. "Just breathe. Relax." He didn't even ask why I was such a mess.

"I can't!" I moaned. "I'm a nervous wreck."

"I'll be right by your side."

"That makes me anxious, too," I admitted. "I'm glad I know you, but you are very... intimidating."

"Intimidating? How am I intimidating?" His blue eyes twinkled. "I try my best to reassure you."

I looked down, embarrassed. "Well," I finally muttered in a low voice, "you *are* very... handsome."

I could hear the smile in his voice.

"Well, thank you. It's not the first time you've been in my company, though."

"In a way... it is."

I knew without looking that he'd cocked a brow as a retort.

"You've always been my tutor," I began.

"And not your date?"

"Yes."

"Gigi, I'm the one who is honored and humbled to have *you* as *my* date."

I looked up, eyes wide.

"But..." suddenly, my throat was full of cotton, and I couldn't utter another word.

"You're gorgeous," he said.

I worked at swallowing my shock.

He continued softly. "I'm ecstatic that I'm the one who gets to take you out. I'll watch over you and guide you. If you become overwhelmed, it's not a problem. I'm here to help you. In addition, I can't help but think how lucky *I* am to have met *you*." He paused, looking up for a minute. "I want you to know... I'm here to help you, not to take advantage. Truly."

It was several more moments before I could even move.

Gently, he reached out his hand and covered mine. "It'll be a good time," he promised.

I nodded with tears in my eyes.

"Gigi?" he asked softly.

"I – I'm just... so happy and thankful," I finally whispered.

"You deserve the best. Your life is going to change. I'm a lucky man because I can say that I'm able to be a part of it."

I just nodded. I wasn't able to do anything else.

"And I can act like I want to be around you."

"Wh – what do you mean?" I asked.

"I mean I don't have to act all formal. I can be myself."

I nodded and tried my best to focus. Needless to say, we got little accomplished. Liz came into the room haughtily.

"Brittany will not be attending a tutoring session today," she announced briskly.

"Okay, Mrs. Chancellor."

"Your time is up with Gigi."

"We just wound it down, ma'am."

Chance stood to take his leave.

"And it will just be Amber and Gigi with you tomorrow."

"Okay."

"Brittany has another date."

Chance nodded slowly. "Yes, ma'am."

Liz looked at him for a few minutes before finally asking, "What time will you be here tomorrow?"

"I'll pick up the girls at 4:30. I want to take them to eat before we go to the dance."

Liz's eyes widened. Then she turned, and without a word, left.

"Well that was a bit awkward," Chance said and smiled at me.

"Liz is very… well, she has an idea of how things are supposed to go, and when they don't go to plan, everyone knows it."

Chance laughed at that.

"It's true," I said with a lowered voice.

"I can see that."

I stared up into Chance's attractive face.

"Walk me to my car?"

"I – I'll walk you to the door." I shuddered when I thought of Liz's reaction if I ventured outside without her permission.

"I'll take what I can get."

His stunning smile shook me to my core. Oh, he'd smiled at me before, but it had been an innocent smile: one of a tutor to his student. This smile had a much different connotation. It was of a man looking at a woman who intrigued him.

Somehow, I tripped on my way to the door. Chance's arm sneaked out and steadied me before I collided with the wall. I felt his warm fingers through the fabric of my shirt. My body trembled in reaction. Chance slowly turned me into him and held me with both hands.

"You okay?" he asked.

"I – I – Um, yes."

His bright eyes were staring at my lips. I licked them nervously.

Liz's voice barked at me from another room. "Gigi!"

Her raucous shout made me jump so much that I nearly rammed Chance's face.

Chance smiled and held on to me. "Hey," he said. "She's not going to eat you. I promise you that."

My eyes must have flashed with the fear that shot through my body because he said, "Do you want to go with me now, Gigi?"

"I – I can't. You better go. I'll see you tomorrow."

Chance's hand lingered on the skin of my arm before he made any effort to open the door.

"*Gigi!*" Liz barked again.

"Coming," I answered.

Chance said softly, "Tomorrow, Gigi."

"Yes."

Then I turned to answer Liz's beckon.

<><><>

"You think you're scot-free, don't you?" Liz huffed.

"N – No, ma'am!"

"I see the way you've changed!   You've even suckered my daughter into your little act!"

I looked down. No matter what I said, I'd be to blame.

"With that young man INSISTING that you go to this dance, too!"

"Ma'am, I don't want to go."

"You shut your mouth.   I know better!   Now go fix dinner.   I have a special guest coming tonight."

"Yes, ma'am."

I began preparing new potatoes and peas, glazed carrots, and a fresh garden salad while Ethan prepared the grill.

"You better really suck up, girl," Ethan suggested.

I snapped my head to look at him.

"Liz is truly pissed."

I nodded once and popped a cherry tart dessert into the oven to cook. Then I prepared sautéed mushrooms for the steak Ethan was going to grill.

I felt confused. I knew Liz didn't want me to act like a human at all. To her, I was only a slave, a human dog with no will of my own. It really wasn't my fault that the law had stepped in and now I had a glamorous man interested in *me*. She was no longer in control one-hundred percent!

Truly, this was the happiest I could remember feeling in forever. I was semi-human at last. I hummed as I worked.

"Come on in," I heard Liz greet a new arrival. I had just set the table with the china finery and the upscale silverware.

"Liz, you look lovely. It's been a very long time," the new voice said.

"Yes, yes it has," Liz agreed. "And thank you."

A key turned somewhere in my mind, and I felt a swirling mist closing in. That voice... I'd heard it many times before.

"Come, I'll show you to the guest room before we sit down to eat."

I heard them heading down the hall towards the room across from mine. By the time they'd returned, the table was heavy with aromatic foods. My stomach rumbled in response.

I felt the blood drain from my face when I saw the monster from my past materialize. It was *her*, the woman who ruined my life who now stood in front of me.

"I see you recognize Sally," Liz said sweetly.

I couldn't respond. I watched as Sally looked me up and down.

"Cat got your tongue?" Liz chuckled huskily.

"She's well-behaved," Sally noted.

"For the most part, yes," Ethan agreed. "She sure has learned how to cook!"

Brittany and Amber warily watched the exchanges. They weren't sure what to make of the conversation circling around me.

"I'm hungee!" Ashton said, banging his spoon down on his high chair.

"Well, we'd better sit down," Liz invited. Then she commanded, "Gigi, make Ashton's plate."

It was a few moments before the feeling returned to my legs. Involuntarily, I did as I was instructed.

"How's the market?" Liz asked happily.

"Business is good! I've never had a lack of demand," Sally laughed.

"Do you keep in contact with all your... business clients?" Liz asked with humor.

"No, not all, but a majority. I like to see the satisfaction of my customers. It's also good for referrals."

"That's nice to know," Liz responded.

"Yes. Happy customers means good word-of-mouth and also potential return clients."

"Very true," Liz agreed.

Everyone began to eat, and I waited on them.

"I have to say I was surprised when you asked me to come and stay a few days," Sally admitted.

"Oh, I have my reasons," Liz said. She nodded toward me. "We don't need more training, just... reminders."

Just then, it dawned on me what that reason was. Liz was threatening me. If I breathed a word to Chance or anyone else, my brother's freedom was limited. Who knows what kind of a home he'd end up in? At least this one was tolerable, especially of late, but I knew my situation could have been a whole lot worse.

Amber said, "Gigi, you look white as a sheet."

I glanced toward Amber and noticed the look on her face. Her brows were knitted, and a frown was pasted to her lips. I needed a moment, so I turned my back to check on the tart. I took it out of the oven and served it while they finished eating the main course.

"Gigi, is it?" Sally asked. A bite of tart was suspended on her fork. "Nice name. Your cooking is phenomenal."

"Yes, ma'am," I said softly.

I worked to swallow because my mouth was excessively dry.

"Ethan cooked the steaks. She's grilled once, but I wanted to have an experienced hand with guests," Liz said. She winked at Sally.

When the conversation died down, I managed to force a question out."H - how's Lucinda?"

"Why, she's great. Training like a pro."

"*Ohhhh*," said Brittany. "*You're* who I need to contact in the future." She smiled as I whipped my head in her direction.

It seemed like days before the meal finally concluded. I sank into a chair as soon as everyone left. I noticed Amber came back in quickly. She came over and put a gentle hand on my shoulder.

"Are you okay?" she asked.

I looked at her blankly.

"Look, I don't know what's going on, but I'm not stupid. Mom can't do this to you. I won't let her intimidate you anymore."

"Thank you, Amber, but I can't talk now. I have to think about all this."

"I'm here for you. I want to do what's right."

Just then, Liz must have noticed that Amber wasn't present and called for her.

"Look. I'm going to go, but I'll come by your room later, and we can talk."

I simply nodded. It was quite a while before I was able to rise and clean.

Later that night, when Amber came to my room, I was so worked up that I was afraid to talk with her. She sat down on my bed next to me and looked at me. She reached out a hand and touched my arm.

"Amber, I can't talk," I managed to whisper in a barely audible voice.

"That woman across the hall?" She pointed and I nodded.

Amber's face rumpled in an angry reaction, a motherly gesture of protection.

"Gigi, you can talk to me, but I know they've beat you down and you're afraid of something. I swear to you, I will help. I don't want you to be more upset, so I'll go for tonight, but I want to know more. Later. Okay?"

I nodded and watched as my one and only friend quietly shut the door behind her.

<><><>

The next morning, I was up early to cook breakfast. I'd barely slept. How could I... with the Troll from the Three Billy Goats Gruff living under my bridge? Not surprisingly, Liz was smug when she came down the stairs.

"Sally and I are going shopping today," she said, barely looking at me. "I know you have plans, but don't think you can shirk your duties."

"I'm not going."

Liz turned to glare at me. What I thought would make her ecstatic made her glower instead.

"What?" she growled. Her brows were crunched over her eyes and her face reddened.

"I said I'm not going."

In the background, I saw Sally's mouth open in surprise that I dared to disagree with my master.

"You WILL go. I didn't spend a fortune on you to have you make things worse with DFS."

"How would I make things worse? I know you don't want me to go."

"No, I don't, but you *have* to go. You *will* go, and then you'll kindly tell Chance you never want to see him again. That is what I want you to do."

"Why? I still have to tutor."

"I'd say that's their problem."

I hung my head with resignation. Liz certainly was a killjoy, and I didn't have much joy to kill.

"Well?" Liz grunted harshly.

In my peripheral vision, I saw Sally fold her arms over her ample chest.

"Yes, ma'am."

"Now you've gotten Amber all worked up. She's made me let you take half the day off to get dressed up. You are to make her happy and act cheerful. Do not tell her that you and Chance are over."

She waited expectantly.

Finally, I whispered, "Yes, ma'am."

"I didn't hear you."

I could only raise my voice a little bit or it would break. "Yes, ma'am."

"Let the girls sleep in. You clean the kitchen and then warm them breakfast... or lunch whenever they arise."

"Yes, ma'am."

Sally nodded approval at my obedience and dared to smile at me.

When the women, Ethan, and Ashton left, I was alone in the kitchen. The girls were still sleeping. I heard the tide rushing in, and before it could overtake me, I ran to my room. Just as I flung myself on the bed, the flood gates opened.

I curled into a fetal position on my twin bed and let the misery wash over me. Wave after crashing wave, the water pounded my emotions until I was a broken heap on the bed. I didn't realize how much time had passed.

"Gigi?" I heard from somewhere in the dark. "Gigi!"

Suddenly, comforting arms were around me, holding me like I'd never recalled being held before. I could not stop the sobs that racked my body.

"Gigi, what is it, honey?" Amber asked.

"N – nothing," I finally managed.

She continued to stroke my hair and hold me until I calmed.

"Now, I know better than to believe it's nothing. It has something to do with that new woman, Sally, is it? Doesn't it?"

"I can't talk about it," I muttered.

"Can't or won't?" she asked. "I know mother's behind this."

"Please," I begged. "Don't tell her... don't tell her I cried."

"That would give her too much satisfaction, wouldn't it?" she asked hatefully.

I didn't respond.

"Look, Gigi, we are going to have fun tonight. I'll help you do whatever chores Mom left. I want you to wipe your eyes and let's get some cold compresses on you. You have a big night ahead. It's going to be fabulous! Once in a lifetime."

More tears leaked out of my eyes.

"Gigi?"

“I – I don’t want to go.”

“What? Why? You’ve got the most handsome of men... Oh. My. God. I smell mother.”

I shook my head. “I – I have to go, though.”

“Damn straight you have to. So, if you don’t want to go, why do you have to?”

“I, uh, I can’t tell you.”

“All right, then let me guess. That way you didn’t tell me.”

“If you say anything to her, she’ll know I told you.”

“Trust me.”

At my nod, Amber basically pegged what was wrong.

“Mom told you to break it off with Chance and is somehow threatening you with that Sally woman.”

I nodded miserably.

“Bullshit. You’re going, you’re going to have fun, and you will NOT break it off with Chance.”

“I have to, Amber. I don’t have a choice.”

Amber’s mouth was a jagged streak. “I say that’s bullshit,” she repeated. “I’ll blow this whole thing open wide on Mom if she pulls this stunt.”

The wide array of emotions that hit me with that statement rocked my world. Questions flooded my mind. *Would I be reunited with my family if that happened, or would my brother be lost forever? Would I have a chance at life or be transferred into another abusive home?*

“Amber,” I asked in a worried tone.

“Gigi, I’m not going to do anything unless I have to, okay? Let’s take one step at a time. I love my family, but I also hate them right now. No person should be treated the way you are."

I nodded but hurriedly asked, "What if your sister hears us talking?" I wrung my hands nervously.

Amber laughed. "She's not even here. It's just us. She has a lot of beauty appointments today, so she's out of our hair."

"What about you?"

"I have a friend who does hair and makeup. She's bringing an additional friend over for our hair, makeup, and nails." Amber let out an excited giggle. "I just *can't wait* to see how pretty you'll be!"

Princess Orlana

About an hour later, my nerves were calm enough that I was able to rise and work with Amber to complete the chore list. When the doorbell rang, two people entered. Murdoc was a tall, wispy, black man whom I liked immediately. Lauren was his physical opposite. She was on the heavier side but a pretty girl with pixie features.

Amber led us upstairs to the old playroom. It had been transformed into a makeup studio some years back. We sat in two beautician chairs and let our artists assess our features. The dresses were hanging nearby so that colors could be matched.

Murdoc buzzed around me, screaming and throwing his hands in the air when he was happy with his creations. He washed, dried, and twisted my hair until it hung in radiant curls. He glitzed it with a wonderfully smelling spritz.

Then came the make-up. I'd never been allowed to play around with the pretty powders except when I was seven, and that didn't really count. I was curious about what all Murdoc was doing to me. I caught admiring looks from Amber and her friend, Lauren. However, I wasn't allowed to look at myself until I was complete, hours later.

Amber ran down to get a few refreshments. When she returned, she said, "Good news! Dad and Ashton are back, but Mom and Sally won't be here in time to see us before we leave!"

I couldn't hide the relief etched on my face, but Amber's friends didn't act at all curious about her announcement. I guessed that to mean that either they knew everything about my odd situation already, or they just didn't care about our family drama.

I breathed an audible sigh of relief. Amber smiled kindly back.

"Get you a drink, girl, before we start on your nails!" Murdoc instructed.

"Okay," I said. Cautiously, I took a soda from the supply Amber had brought up. It felt so strange to be receiving instead of serving. I took a swallow then asked, "Murdoc, are you going to the dance?"

"I didn't have time to dress shop," he said, and we all laughed with him.

"How about you, Lauren?" I asked shyly.

"Naw," she responded with a smile. "The Bachelor is on tonight."

"Honey, nothing can take the place of that show!" Murdoc said, laughing.

"I know, right?" she agreed.

We all laughed again.

I watched as Murdoc prepared my nails. He somehow created a glittery creation from the canvas of my nails. They began a vibrant fuchsia that melted into pink. The pink faded into white brilliance. A dazzling layer of glitter covered the darkest pink and lightened as the color dissipated. All I could do was watch and drink in all the beauty. I felt as if I were in some sort of dream. I truly felt like a princess... *like Orlana!*

We donned our gowns just as the door rang. I was very nervous, but the glamour gave me the shell of confidence I needed. Normally, I would never have been able to walk down those stairs on my own, in finery fit for a queen, when the most handsome of men would be waiting and watching.

"Amber, thank you for such a magical day! You look so beautiful!" I breathed. "I've never had so much fun. I can never thank you enough!"

We embraced in a sisterly hug.

"Gigi, it is you who looks magnificent!" she cried. "I'm going to show you what *you* look like now!"

She brought me before a covered full-length mirror. When she unveiled the piece, the woman standing before me simply could not be me. I looked for Gigi, but she simply wasn't there. My mouth dropped open in shock, and so did the princess's in the mirror.

Amber was grinning widely. "Surprised?" she asked.

"Is... that... me?" I croaked.

"Oh, honey! You like my work?" Murdoc asked with a Cheshire grin.

"Who wouldn't?" Lauren breathed. "You're naturally beautiful, Gigi, but Murdoc knows how to showcase it!"

I continued to stare. My hair was spun in gold ringlets down my back. The sides were pulled up into a loose bun which overflowed and spilled down to blend in with the rest of the loose curls. A few free tendrils twisted gently to frame my face. The tiny tiara on top gleamed brilliantly.

My eye shadow reflected the pink in my dress but was accented by a hint of electric blue which accentuated and made my eyes appear more alive. My lashes, long and luxurious, didn't seem to be real. In addition, the silvery pink dress brought out my creamy complexion and accented the pink in my cheeks and lips. A bedazzled necklace and matching earrings completed the picture.

All I could do was stare. Murdoc *could* perform miracles. This young woman simply could not be me.

"Stunning, huh?" asked Amber gleefully.

"Wow," I said. "I'll bet your mom wouldn't recognize me," I said with a laugh.

Amber laughed, too, and said, "Now we know how to sneak you out for fun right in plain sight."

"Amber, you look like a princess, too!" I said happily.

Amber's golden gown was the perfect reflection for her, as well. The sheath dress was barely discernible under the sheer white and molten gold layers of fabric. The dress was certainly fitted, but it was the perfect amount of elegance to show off Amber's body without being too risqué. The bodice was molded over her chest, but it didn't dip too low. Tiny brilliant diamonds danced iridescently from the folds of cloth.

"Thank you, Gigi." She smiled gently at me. "Are you ready?"

"No," I whispered.

"Well, Princess, ready or not..."

We began descending the stairs. I saw Chance near the bottom of the stairs standing by Ethan. He was dressed in a black tuxedo with a pale pink cumberbun. He looked the part of a dashing prince who had the heart of every nearby maiden.

The looks on the menfolk below was all the proof we needed to know we were breathtaking. Chance couldn't take his eyes off me. Even Ethan was spellbound.

"Da-da, who dat?" Ashton asked, pointing.

"I really don't know, son," Ethan replied in awe.

When we got down the stairs, I went directly to Chance.

Ethan kissed his daughter, then we followed Chance out the door.

"Here's the limo," he offered.

Chance directed me by placing a light hand under my elbow. I nearly choked when I saw the chauffeur open the door for us. Mr. Ponder was dressed as any well-paid chauffeur would be. He wore a black evening suit accented by a crisp white shirt, gloves, and black tie. His eyes twinkled at me from under the dark driving hat.

"Madam," he said as he swung the stylish door open for me. Lustrous light shimmered down the side of the pearl paint.

Mr. Ponder went to the other side and did the same for Amber. Chance sat between us, and the limo pulled out from the drive.

"Miss Amber," Mr. Ponder began, "Where next?"

Amber recited an address. My eyes flew to her, full of questions.

"We're picking up my date, now," she said laughing. "I thought we could double date instead of me being the third wheel as Mom would like."

Chance chuckled at her words, but his blue eyes were still glued to me.

"Afterwards, we'll go to dinner," Chance finally said. He turned to Amber. "Tonight, Gigi isn't Gigi."

"I agree!" she said, "She's a completely new creation based on the old. She's beautiful no matter what, but now we've added a layer of glamour."

"Yes, and tonight, Gigi's name is Zoey. Are you okay with that?"

"Yes," Amber said, slightly surprised.

"But please don't tell your mom," I pleaded.

"You bet," she replied. "Heaven forbid we go against anything Mom calls you."

When we arrived at the address, Mr. Ponder opened the door for Amber then closed it and waited by the car while she went to retrieve her date.

"You are simply stunning," Chance uttered in my ear when we were alone.

"I – I... Um, thank you," I said.

He turned his body toward me, and I was mesmerized by his crystalline blues. We stared at one another for a few moments before our faces broke into smiles.

Just then, light flooded into the vehicle as the two other occupants joined us inside.

"Whoa, what's going on in here?" Amber teased.

I must have appeared flustered, because Chance whispered in my ear, "She's teasing you. You don't have to answer."

When Mr. Ponder began driving, Amber said, "This is my date, Josh. Josh, this is Chance and Zoey."

"Nice to meet you," he said.

Josh was of average height from what I could tell. His warm brown eyes glinted with peace, and his smile was disarming.

"Likewise," Chance greeted.

I held out a hand and smiled. "I'm so happy you're going with us," I said.

We visited as the lavish vehicle took us to an upscale Italian restaurant.

"I sure hope I don't make a mess of myself," I laughed nervously.

"Me, too!" Amber agreed.

"Just be careful about what you order," Josh suggested.

"Definitely," Chance added.

The meal went well, and everyone escaped relatively mess-free. Mr. Ponder footed the bill.

"Thank you, Mr. Ponder," I said. Everyone else thanked him, too.

"You're welcome, all of you."

We pulled up to the ornate church that Project Graduation had reserved for the dance. The castle-like building had donated its use to add to the magical theme. The brownstone *did* resemble a palace. My heart was beating hard in nervous anticipation.

"Now, you kids go have fun. Chance, let me know when you're all ready to go." Mr. Ponder held up his hand and waved his cell phone.

Chance nodded as Mr. Ponder held the door.

"My lady?" He proffered a hand.

I put mine in his, and Chance helped me from the car. We waited as Mr. Ponder did the same for Amber and Josh.

I squeezed Chance's hand, and we all went to the door. The entrance was picturesque and welcoming. A table of parent chaperones took our money to enter.

"Ooohh," they exclaimed at us. "You certainly came to the right place! What are your names, dearies? You *have* to enter the princess contest!"

"You can put Amber and Zoey Chancellor down," Amber said, eyeing the prize. The winner would be crowned with a magnificent tiara and scepter. Both were encrusted with brilliant white diamonds. There was also a huge bouquet of sophisticated blood-red roses on slender deep green stems.

"Wow," I mouthed to Chance. His huge grin swallowed my fright. I was feeling happy and more confident.

We entered into the main foyer of the church, and the decorations were extravagant. One might expect a tad cheesy atmosphere if high schoolers attended a Orlana dance, but this was done in style. The decorations were so authentic that if I didn't know better, a swarm of butterfly and moth faeries would be arriving for the annual ball.

I looked around in awe. Chance was happy guiding me so that I didn't stumble because I was certainly not paying attention to where I was walking. I knew that my eyes had to be giant saucers absorbing all the world had to offer. It wasn't often the dog was let out of its cage!

"Zoey, let's grab a drink. Then I want to dance with you," Chance said into my ear.

I looked up into his striking features and said, "I'd like that very much."

We grabbed drinks and sat at a nearby table. Josh and Amber joined us. I continued to stare until the surroundings finally began to take on a hue of reality. Chance just watched me taking it all in.

Amber smiled and asked, "Are you enjoying yourself, Zoey?"

"Yes, very much!" I exclaimed.

"I'm glad. You deserve this and so much more," she said softly.

"She's in store for a lot more excursions," Chance agreed.

With his statement, I tried not to let the anxiety overtake me. Liz's order to break up with Chance kept resounding in my head.

"Stop it," Amber ordered.

"Stop what?" I asked.

"Stop thinking about Mom. I'll handle her. Her overbearing control-freaking is done! I swear it!"

"Amber..."

"Okay. Let's not talk... or think... of Mom tonight. Deal?"

"But, she – "

"Zoey."

All three of my companions stared at me with stern expressions.

"Oh, okay," I sighed. I made a gallant effort to release my anxiety.

"Come on," Chance said. "Our drinks can wait. Let's dance!" and with that, Mr. Tall, Dark, and Handsome pulled me onto the floor.

Almost in correlation, a new song flooded onto the surface and swirled around us in romantic bliss. Chance's eyes twinkled as he enveloped me in his arms.

"It's okay," he reassured. "You're safe in my arms."

I looked into his mesmerizing eyes. He was so handsome and strong... and close.

"I – I know," I whispered.

"Relax. Move to the music. It's natural."

While we danced, someone rammed into my back: we'd collided with another couple.

I cried out softly in surprise.

"Oh, I'm *so* sorry," a voice sneered from behind me. "I didn't see you there."

I'd have fallen if Chance hadn't been still holding me in his arms. I turned to look and nearly fell a second time from Brittany's aura of hate that enveloped me.

She continued, "I see you're having fun." Her eyes raked me up and down and her lip curled in distaste.

Brittany was dressed in her deep crimson mermaid gown inlaid with gold piping and sprinkled with wine-colored and gilded sequins. Its V-neckline dipped down into her ample cleavage. The dress clung to her figure and flared at all the appropriate places. The gold hemline peeked from under a layer of the blood red fabric. Gold and ruby earrings laughed at me from her ears, and I almost couldn't tear my eyes from the necklace nestled between her uplifted breasts.

Brittany's heavy make-up and matching red lipstick almost made her difficult to recognize. Her lashes were thick and false. There was no denying her beauty, but it felt as fake as she was.

"Yes, thank you," I managed to say.

"I may take a dance later," she informed Chance almost huffily. "We need to talk."

Without awaiting a response, she twirled, leading a surprised-looking Blake away. I noticed Blake still staring at me and Brittany's haughty response.

"Are you all right?" Chance asked. His brows had lowered with the encounter.

"She surprised me more than she hurt me," I said.

"She managed to knock you quite forcefully," he replied stubbornly.

"I'm okay," I said. I paused a second before adding, "Are you... going to dance with her?"

His displeasure disappeared, and a slow, sexy smile erupted from his lips.

"Not if you don't want me to," he said.

"Do you *want* to?" I asked indignantly. Without meaning to, I felt a brow raise.

"No, I do not. Why would I want to dance with anyone else when the most beautiful girl is in my arms?"

He melted my heart with that statement. "Th –
thank you, Chance," and I wasn't really talking about
the compliment.

Chance grinned and let me back to our table.

"So, was that my sister that rammed into you?"
Amber asked. Her brows were rumpled over glittering
eyes. Without waiting for confirmation, she said,
"She's just like Mother!"

"It's okay," I murmured. "But she told Chance
she wanted to dance with him later."

"Like hell."

"My feelings exactly. She can 'bump' into me all
she likes, but she's not dancing with…"

I felt all three people's eyes on me.

"Were you going to say…" Chance began.

Amber waited a beat before adding, "My man'?"

I blushed furiously and looked down. Amber
began laughing out loud.

"You're a hoot," she said. "And that wasn't just a
bump, but I'll let you two talk a few. Come on,
Josh. It's our turn to dance!"

"I can put Brittany in her place eloquently,"
Chance said once they'd left. "I don't want any more
trouble for you than there has to be."

"I'm sure she's going to say something terrible
about m – me," my voice wavered.

"Zoey? You know I have my own eyes to see with,
right?"

I nodded.

"And my own ears to hear with?"

Again, I acknowledged him.

"Don't you think I can see what's going on here? Probably more than you want me to see, but I know. We're here to have fun, and nothing she says gets to stop that. Understand?"

"Yes."

"Okay, then. Grab a drink, and we can dance some more, if you'd like?"

I could only nod as he stood and held out his hand to me.

After another hour of dancing and having fun with Josh and Amber, the women that took our tickets proclaimed that they would be announcing the winner of the Orlana contest after the next song.

"I'm scared," I whispered to Amber, Josh, and Chance.

"Don't be," Chance said.

"You're a naturally-born princess," Amber agreed. "I hope you get it."

"I think someone else has a mind for it," Josh said and gestured with a flip of his hand.

Brittany was strolling around, trying to gain the attention of the judges.

Amber laughed. "I think it'd be hilarious if Zoey did get it! Brittany would have a *fit*!"

My face must have paled, because she said, "Girl, you're safe. I'm a true advocate now. I've been silent waaay too long."

Chance cocked a brow.

"Yes, I would like to meet with you about this," Amber said. "But not here, not now."

"I appreciate that," he admitted.

"Don't I have a say in all this?" I croaked.

"Yes. Let's talk *later*," Amber conceded.

We watched as Brittany and Blake danced across the floor. Their moves teetered on over-the-line but stayed right on the border. I wondered vaguely if that was her last-ditch effort to gain the judge's attention.

When the song ended, two women and a man announcer walked up onto the stage. A drum roll began, and big spotlights of different colors circled and zoomed over the crowd and floor.

"And now," the male announcer's voice began. "The moment we've all been waiting for! The winner of the Orlana title. This victor has been chosen on the following merits: A) Appearance – who has a similar manner of dressing gown; B) Mannerisms – which lady is most demure; and C) Couple – which couple appears most like a prince and princess overall."

The crowd screamed in response.

"And the princess to claim the title of Miss Orlana is..."

The drums rolled dramatically.

The sing-song voice drew out the name: "Miss Zoey Chancellor!"

"Oh, my God! Zoey!" yelled Amber. "You've done it! You've won!" She jumped up and down a few times in her excitement.

"Me?" I croaked.

Orlana? There was so much symbolism in that word, in that character, and now I was deemed as noble enough to carry the title? I was overwhelmed.

"Come on, love," Chance said, helping me to my feet.

I clutched at his muscular arm because I knew my own legs wouldn't support my weight without his assistance.

We slowly made our way toward the center stage at the end of the dance floor. Teens parted to allow us passage. The spotlights were trained on us as we made our way.

When I somehow got on the stage, Chance continued to be my rock. In a flurry of movement, my small tiara was replaced with the larger one, and I was given the scepter and bouquet. Cameras were flashing at us. We walked back and forth a few times while the crowd yelled and whistled in appreciation.

"Princess Orlana and Prince Terren, will you honor us with a dance on stage?" the announcer asked.

A lady came to retrieve my roses and staff while we led the dance. Chance enveloped me in his strength, and his arms came around me as the music began. I was lost to the world from within his embrace. We began to sway with the melody. No longer did I feel the world was staring at me. Chance was my knight in shining armor, and I felt I could face the world with him at my side.

When the dance finished, Chance played his part. He lowered his head and placed a gentle kiss on me in front of the multitude. Screams of support erupted around us. Tonight, we really were the Faery Tale Land characters personified. My heart swelled with adoration.

The Biggest Surprise of All

When the kiss ended, Chance cradled my face in his warm hands.   He huskily uttered, "Your surprises aren't over."

Chance led me off the stage.   The lady brought my possessions to our table. Chance's phone buzzed, and he looked at it briefly then smiled.

"Let's go outside and get some fresh air, okay?" he asked.

"Y – yes," I agreed, mildly wondering if something else could be going on.

Amber and Josh joined us.   As we were leaving, a hateful voice cut through the crowd.

"Congratulations, uh, *Zoey*."

I didn't even try to find the source of the voice.   I wouldn't give Brittany the satisfaction.

The refreshing night air filled my lungs and calmed me.   Chance punched a text into his phone.

"Your surprise should be pulling up shortly," he said.   Then he drew Amber aside and whispered conspiratorially into her ear.

She squealed a response and jumped up and down.

Seconds later, I heard tires turning into the circular drive in front of the church.   It was the pearly white limo.

"Are we going somewhere?" I asked nervously.

"You'll see!" Amber said excitedly.

Mr. Ponder got out of the driver's seat and opened the doors of the luxury vehicle.   A man, woman, and teenaged boy emerged. Suddenly, I was in the middle of arms that hugged and squeezed me. Someone was keening with deep emotion. I realized the sound was coming from me. I was crying like my soul was leaving my body.

"Mom! Dad! Brycen! How? How did you find me?" and before they could answer, I kept repeatedly yelling, "I can't believe it! I can't believe it!"

It was the best day in my entire life. When the excitement finally abated, I repeated, "Mom, Dad, how did you find me?"

"We owe our thanks to this man," Daddy said and put a hand on Mr. Ponder's shoulder.

"Mr. Ponder? *How?*"

"Young lady, when Chance and I talked that day we left the Chancellor's house... remember when he offered to take all three of you girls to this dance?"

I nodded.

"Well, I offered to be the chauffeur. I also drive a limo on the weekends to supplement my income. I told him that I thought it would be a great way to support you and make you feel more comfortable on a date... of sorts. When Chance revealed to me what you wanted your name to be on your night of freedom, I decided to research missing reports of Zoeys that were in your age group within the state."

"I, uh, might have told him your real age, too," Chance said. "I wanted to help as much as I could."

"You never gave me a clue," I said.

"If I had, you'd have been so full of anxiety that you couldn't have hidden it from the Chancellors. Now isn't that true?"

"Yes."

Mr. Ponder continued, "When I found the family I believed to be yours, I reached out to them with the hope that they were the ones. They were on-board to meet you."

"Zoey, when we saw your picture, we knew it was you," Mama said, "It was so hard to wait until tonight to have you in our arms again."

We all hugged again.

"What picture, Mom?" I truly was confused. I glanced over at Chance.

"Uh, I sort of took one of you with my phone. I thought it could help in our search. I hope you don't mind."

"How could I be angry about that now?" I asked.

I turned to my brother. "Brycen, you've grown so much! I have missed you more than I can ever tell you."

"Zoey, I've missed you so much, too," he said, grabbing me again.

Mr. Ponder said, "In addition, your kidnappers are being picked up and taken to police headquarters. They'll be arrested and detained for questioning."

"*What?*" asked Amber.

"Did you manage to get Sally?" I squeaked.

"Sally?" Mr. Ponder asked.

"She's the lady that was visiting them. She's the one who actually kidnapped me," I said. "I overheard them talking that she still has a 'booming business' of rehoming the children she steals."

Mr. Ponder whipped out his phone and was on it faster than I could believe. Then I glanced over at Amber. She looked like a train wreck. I saw happiness for me, sadness for her parents, and fright for herself. I reached out to console her.

"Amber, are you okay?"

"Ah, I don't know, Zoey. I mean, sure. I know this had to stop, but... I know what Mom and Dad's done is wrong on so many levels. I guess I'm just... scared. Scared for me and Ashton. And Brittany, scared for her, too."

"I can understand," I said, honestly. "But don't worry. We'll figure something out."

"You'll have a warm home to go to. They won't throw you out in the cold," Chance reassured.

"What about my brother? My sister? I - I just... I'm scared. What am I going to do? I know I'm legally an adult, but... I'm still in high school. I don't have the money to pay for our house. I'm not ready to be a parent to my baby brother, but I sure as heck can't let him go anywhere else. And I know that Brittany isn't any better prepared than I am." She paced. "She's in college, and she isn't patient at all. You *know* that. I mean, what will we do without our parents? No," she said and shook her head, "I'll definitely have to be the one to care for Ashton."

Mr. Ponder cut in, "We've made arrangements for you and your brother."

"What about Brittany?" Amber managed.

Mr. Ponder said, "Brittany's legally an adult. She can stay with friends or other family members. Unfortunately, once a child has reached adult status, there's little we can do besides point them in the direction of services we offer."

Amber nodded miserably. "But, I'm legally an adult, too."

"Yes, but I have a friend that will take you in anyway, if you're willing. She does foster care, so she knows what she's doing. *You* won't be fostered, of course. You're eighteen, but you're still in high school. She will provide for you. We can get you in for your brother's sake because it's in his best interest. In essence, we're allowing you to stay with him for *his* benefit. We're kinda bending rules, but it gets you in and we can list her as the provider for your brother on the paperwork."

Amber nodded but looked miserable.

"I'm sorry, Amber," I whispered. I wrapped my arms around her. Although my heart was soaring with happiness, it hurt for her.

"Don't worry," Mr. Ponder said. "We'll take good care of her."

Amber nodded but I saw tears glimmering in her eyes. "Mr. Ponder, if you'll excuse me, I need to tell Brittany what's going on. She needs time to figure out what to do. Zoey, I love you and I'm happy for you, but I'll talk to you later. I've got to figure all this out."

We hugged and said a teary goodbye. Amber disappeared back into the building while my family enveloped me with arms again.

"Zoey," Mom said, "I still can't believe it. I got my baby back."

"I know, Mom. Dad, I've missed you so much. I can't even explain," I said and squeezed her again.

We continued to mutter happiness at finding each other once again.

I kept staring at Brycen. I couldn't believe how much my brother had changed. I clutched him in my arms. I didn't think I could ever let go of him again.

Home Is Where the Heart Is

When we arrived back at my real home, I felt like I was taking a trip down memory lane. It was so strange to see all my childhood memories through adult eyes. My room was still decorated with an Orlana theme. The pink walls were definitely more suited to an eight-year-old girl, but I was happy to be back in it. I saw my birthday wand. It was in a framed case hanging on my wall. A lump swelled in my throat.

"We, um, didn't change much," Mama said.

"We couldn't stand to," Daddy said.

"Just in case you ever came home," Mama finished.

"I understand," I said, "And... I'm finally home!"

We grinned at one another.

"Can... we make popcorn and have a night watching movies?" I asked. "I... just want to spend as much time with you as I can. And, well, I haven't had any... um, time to watch anything. So whatever we watch really will be the first time I get to see it."

My family froze momentarily as my innocent statement swept over them.

Brycen said, "I'd like that, sis," and wrapped his arms around me.

My parents nodded.

"Go pick out a movie, honey," Daddy said.

"I'll start the popcorn," Mom said.

<><><>

In the morning, I knocked on Brycen's door.

"Hey," I said.

"Hey, Sis. Come on in."

I sat on the edge of his bed. He was perched in front of his television with a paused game.

"I've missed you so much," Brycen said.

"And I, you. I've thought of you so much through the years. I want to know all about you. Who you are now, and what you do in your free time."

He glanced toward the monitor.

I laughed. "I'm sure there's a lot more to you than a video game or two. I want to know what your other interests are, who your friends are, what you like to do in your spare time, what college you want to go to, and, well, just *everything*."

"I want to know as much as I can about you and your life, too, sis," Brycen said. "That is what you can tell me. I don't want to make you relive any trauma, but I want to know everything, everything you can or are willing to share. I want to know your likes, dislikes, and *all* about you, as well."

For the next several hours, we talked. I relayed what my life had been like, but I tried to spare the most awful experiences. In turn, Brycen shared his life with me.

"So, sis, I'm glad you've had a few people who've treated you well in that horrible time. I think you should talk to Mom about how you feel about Amber. I know she's staying with her baby brother who's in foster care and that she's eighteen, but maybe we can help her more than we are now."

"That's a good idea, Brycen. I'll talk to her about some ideas running around in my head. I mean, graduation is only a few weeks away. I know she can get custody of Ashton fairly easily once she is seen as an adult in the eyes of the system."

"I think that would be great. Maybe even talk to her about Lucinda... and fill her in on what your life was like not only with the Chancellors but also with Sally. She'll hate to hear it, yet she needs to know. Your life was bad, to be sure, but sis, it could have been worse, by a lot. Mom won't want to hear how badly you were treated, but it will relieve her, all at the same time."

"I know, Brycen. I don't want anyone to feel sorry for me, but I suppose it'll be good for me to get it out. I want to help Amber, and oh, man, I'd love to find Lucinda. She'll need help even more than I do, if we can locate her."

Epilogue

"Amber, you and Ashton can settle in this room, if you'd like," Mom said. She led them into a large room that we saved for our welcomed guests.

"Our home is more modest than what you're accustomed to," Dad said, "but we have plenty of room for all of you. We can get downstairs remodeled for you and your brother if you don't mind staying here, in this room, until arrangements can be made."

Amber smiled. "That's more than generous, Mr. and Mrs. Lovette. Thank you."

"We can never thank you enough for showing kindness to our Zoey. And please. I'm Eva."

"And Aden, at your service."

Dad gave a small bow. We giggled.

"Thank you, again. I can't tell you how much I appreciate your generosity."

"You're welcome here as long as you want or need," Dad said.

"Nuestro casa es su casa," Mom said.

Amber smiled. "Gracias, señora."

"I mean, as *long* as you want," Dad reiterated.

She stepped into the room and began to unpack.

"I'll watch Ashton while you make yourself at home," I offered.

"Why don't you help me, and then you can give me a guided tour?" Amber asked.

I gave her a happy hug and nodded.

"So... I have to ask. Is Brittany okay?"

Amber looked at me. "Yes, but she wouldn't agree with me. Uncle Ajay and Aunt Margaret took her in, but they struggle more with finances. They have enough money to take her in, but not with all the finery she's accustomed to."

"I hope she realizes what it would be like if she didn't have a place to go."

"Is that a nice way of saying she better keep her mouth shut and not complain?"

I grinned. "Maybe. I'm relieved to hear she is okay, though."

"Yes. Thank you for asking. I don't agree with how spoiled she is, but I love her anyway."

I nodded. "Family has to stick together."

<><><>

"Zoey? Get ready to load up," Dad said. "I'll pull the car around."

"Really? We're going to go?" I asked.

"Yes, honey," Mom said. "We know how important this is to you."

"Thank you, Mom and Dad. It really means a lot."

The drive to the airport was only about forty minutes, but it seemed like forever. We handed our tickets to the flight attendant. It would be a short flight, from one end of the state to the other.

"We'll be landing in Miami. It'll still be a bit of a drive to go to the exact spot in the Everglades," Dad said.

264

"Thank you," I said, leaning in to him. "You don't know how much it means. Your willingness to take in Amber and Ashton, and now Lucinda. Both of you. But... you know she's a lot older than me and has never had a good life."

"We missed out on so much of *your* life, honey," Mom said. "We want to give you as much as we can. We missed out, but you did even more so."

Dad said, "And we've talked to Mr. Ponder about some possible things we can do to help Lucinda if we can get her to come with us. Some support groups, counseling, that kind of thing. Zoey, it's going to be hard for her... adjusting. She's quite a bit older than you, and from what you've told us, she's never had a loving home. She's never had freedom to speak of. It's not going to be a walk in the park."

I nodded. "I know. Believe me, I know. It's not easy for me, and she's been more exposed to abuse than me." I paused, then asked tentatively, "It *is* just Lucinda there, right?"

"Yes, honey," Mom said.

"They rescued the children already. I hear they're already reunited with their families," Dad said.

"What about Nick?"

No one said anything for a few moments.

Dad broke the silence by saying, "He escaped. They're on the lookout for him."

"Poor Lucinda. I know she has to be terrified."

"We have plenty of space. If Amber and Ashton live in the basement, she can have the guest room. Or we could even add another room down there. It'll be like an apartment for whoever wants to have space down there," Mom said.

"I just hope she wants to come with us," I said. "This has been her life for, well, forever. She'll be even more socially awkward than me."

"We're here to help as much as we can," Dad said. "But ultimately, the choice is hers, Zoe."

"I know."

We turned into that long lonely drive. My heart rate picked up. No matter how much time had passed, it felt as if the trauma was currently happening. That car, the Orlana dress, Nick, and Sally. The horror of realizing what was happening. That I'd never see my family again... even if they were sitting right next to me.

As soon as we parked, the front door opened, and Lucinda stepped out onto the porch. All the years we were apart flew away. I ran to her and she opened her arms wide. We fell into each other's arms, sobbing.

"Oh, Lucinda!"

"Zoey! How I've missed you!"

"I've missed you so dreadfully! Oh, my goodness. It's so good to see you."

"Yes, Zoey. I've thought about you night and day since you left. When I heard Sally was going to see you, well, I cried. I wanted to come and at the same time, I didn't want you to feel those feelings again when you saw her."

I just nodded, hiccuping. When I pulled back, I looked into her face. "Lucinda, these are my parents. My Dad, Aden Lovette, and my Mom, Eva Lovette."

"Nice to meet you, Lucinda," my mom said, reaching out a hand.

"We're deeply indebted to you for all that you've done for Zoey," Dad said.

"Lucinda? Would you... would you come back and stay with us?" I asked.

Lucinda looked around and said, "And leave all this?"

I snorted a laugh. "Well, it's familiar."

"And hated."

"You're sure?"

Lucinda looked at my parents. "Yes. Thank you, Mr. and Mrs. Lovette. Truly. I just, well, I have no money or support. It's just me and a few belongings. I can clean for you to pay for my way, or I can get a job.."

"We'll work it out," Mom said. "Getting you to safety is the priority. The details will work themselves out."

"We also have other house guests," I said. "Amber, the girl that's my age, and her younger brother are also staying with us. You'll love them. She's struggling with all that her parents have done, but together, we'll all heal. I just know it."

We hugged again and got into the car.

A few days later, I was standing in my pink room, holding different samples of paint up against the wall.

"Sis?" Brycen's deepened voice called me.

"Yes?"

"Your phone is ringing."

"Really? I can't hear it."

Brycen laughed. "You left it on silent again." He brought the device over to me. "You might want to get it. It's Chance."

I snatched the cell from my brother's hand and watched his grin deepened.

"Hello?"

"Hey," Chance said. "It's so great to talk to you on the phone... finally."

"I know, right? Now if I can figure this silly thing out. I think it is smarter than I am."

"I know that's not true. So, how're you doing?"

"Fine," I said. I didn't know what to say, so I blurted out what was on my mind. "Chance? Would you still... tutor me?"

"Of course. I love donating my time to a worthy cause," he chuckled.

"Donating? I'm sure my parents can pay you."

"Zoey, I think they've got enough on their plates. They're taking in three additional people to care for. Please, it's the least I can do. Plus, I get to spend time with you."

Although he couldn't see me, I could feel my face warm, and I smiled.

"Are you blushing?" he asked.

"Maybe."

"I'd also... like to see you. I mean, date you, when you're ready. We can move very slowly. The nice thing, if you're willing, is we no longer need Liz's approval."

"I'd really like that, Chance."

"Great! I'll see you on Monday."

"It's a date."

"Really?" he asked.

"I, uh, meant... for tutoring."

Chance laughed. "I'm teasing you. I'll be there at 10:30."

"I can't wait."

"Me either, Zoey. I'm so happy for you."

"I am, too, Chance. You're a big part of the reason I've been reunited with my family."

"I only played a very small part. The real wonder worker is Mr.-"

"-Ponder," we said together.

"Yes, the man is a saint," I said. "I'll always be thankful to him, but honestly... I'm really looking forward to seeing you," I whispered.

"I feel the same. Soon, Zoey, soon."

"Monday."

"Right."

We said our goodbyes, and I hung up.

I laid back on my bed, happier than I could remember. I would never take the gift of love and family for granted again. My thoughts touched on the tale that had woven itself through the fabric of my life. I felt I truly was Orlana, the Golden Faery Queen.

*If you liked this story, *The Other Side of Privileged,* I would greatly appreciate a positive review. The following site(s), especially Goodreads, would be very helpful.   Thank you.

Goodreads
Barnes and Noble
Amazon
Wal*Mart

Orlana, the Golden Faery Queen

By Sheri Chapman

Edited by Eric Myers

Illustrated by Aadil Khan

This children's book was inspired by my story, The Other Side of Privileged.   I wrote this short story to coincide with the longer, darker themed book. Several people enjoyed the tale, and it inspired me to try my hand at my first book for children.   I hope you enjoy.

Orlana, the Golden Faery Queen

Edited by Eric Myers
Illustrated by Aadil Khan

Once upon a time, in Faery Tale Land, there lived the king and queen of faeries. They were a good couple and ruled with kindness and love. They only used their magic to help, protect, or heal those in their kingdom.

One day, King Oberon and Queen Tania had a baby. They named her Orlana, and she was the future Golden Queen.

The day of her birth was so bright, everyone had to wear sunglasses. It was a sign of great fortune. The butterfly lords all came to pay their respects along with other fae folk. They bestowed rare and wonderful gifts on the baby girl.

King Kheelan, Lord of the Moth Faeries, was jealous of King Oberon. Everyone seemed to value King Oberon as the high lord of the all the kings in the faery realm.

In the tales of old, there was a story of a queen who would rise up. Her golden light would run all the moth faeries into the darkest recesses of the world. It would end their games of fun with the non-magical folk. There would be no more tricks or ploys to protect the magical realm. All the leprechauns and dwarfs, along with their riches, would disappear forever. Only the good faeries would remain.

Partly out of anger because the presentation of Orlana happened on a day he could not attend and partly because of the story of old, King Kheelan swore he would stop the prophecy from coming true.

That night, he and a gathering of arrow-winged faeries flew to the castle of King Oberon. They brought the Ring of Darkness with them. When they reached baby Orlana, they slipped the

Ring of Darkness onto her wrist, disguising her, and took her far away.

King Oberon and Queen Tania were very distraught. They looked and looked for their baby girl. They sent out all the fae and wildlife they could to help them look. Even the butterfly lords and spirits of the trees looked for the future golden queen, but it was to no avail.

Orlana was put in a cave dungeon close to the sea. The Ring of Darkness overpowered her gift of golden light. It was said that only a tap from her glitter wand or the kiss of her one true love could shatter the ring and release her light onto the world.

Many years passed. Orlana hadn't seen daylight since her abduction. To keep her busy and watch over her, Orlana was taken, only in the cover of night, to two of the moth lord's homes to clean. Before every dawn, she was returned to her cave dungeon home.

In her adolescent years, King Kheelan's wife became jealous of the serving girl, so Orlana was sent to clean for Lord Flyn and stayed with the family full-time.

It was a very lonely life. Orlana was sad, but the golden light, deep inside her, provided hope.

Orlana hated the Ring of Darkness. It was heavy and cold against her skin. It kept her in a bubble that somehow controlled her radiance. No one could really see the bubble, but Orlana could feel it.

One day, the King Oberon announced he would be hosting the yearly ball so that all the single fae could meet others of their kind. It was to start in the evening and continue on into the night to accommodate both the daylight and nocturnal fae.

Sibelle, the daughter of Lord Flyn, was very mean to Orlana. She insisted that the princess wait on her hand and foot. Sibelle was an avid lover of fae fashion, and had many beautiful gowns. Still, she still insisted on a new one and forced Orlana to prepare her for the dance.

"Papa, I need Orlana to come to the ball with me," she said.

"That is not allowed," Lord Flyn said.

"But why? The Ring of Darkness will keep her true identity a secret. All who look see only a dark-haired servant girl."

"I suppose that is true."

"Can I bring her? Please?" Sibelle begged.

"I suppose. I will go to watch over you. If there is any sign of trouble, I will take her back to the cave dungeon to hide until it is safe. Do you understand and agree?"

"Oh, yes, Papa."

And so Orlana was allowed to attend the ball. Sibelle gave the princess one of her older dresses to wear, but it was still beautiful on the girl.

When the family arrived, many were there, already dancing. It was customary for the day fae to begin the ball where the night fae would dance throughout the night.

"Go get me a drink," Sibelle said.

"Yes, Lady Sibelle," Orlana said.

She weaved her way through the crowd. To onlookers, her hair was an inky black that spiraled down her back, and her wings were as dark as obsidian.

At times, though, a ripple of light would hint at a touch of glitter on the dark feathers.

Orlana plucked a flute of lavender bubbly liquid from a passing server. At the same time, a man with dark hair reached for a glass. He bumped her arm but was able to grab her wrist to steady the drink before it spilled. His eyes widened in astonishment.

"Hello," he said, looking down into her falsely colored eyes.

"H - hello," she said.

"I am Prince Terren of the Realm of Toleran."

"I - I am just a serving girl, my lord," she said with a curtsy of respect.

"What is your name?" he asked.

"My name is... Abella," Orlana said. "I must go, my lord. My lady is waiting."

Orlana pushed through the crowd until she reached Sibelle's side.

"What took you so long?" she asked with narrowed eyes.

"It is very crowded, my lady. I have never seen so many fae."

"Huh," she said. She picked up the glass and drained it. "I'll need another."

"Yes, my lady."

Orlana turned to go and found the same serving man. Prince Terren was there as well, much where she'd left him. He watched her approach.

Nervously, she plucked another flute from a tray.

"Take one for yourself," the prince said, catching up to her.

"I cannot, my lord."

"Take two, then, for your lady."

Orlana giggled. "That is a good idea, kind sir."

He handed her another.

"In fact, let's take an entire tray."

The next server that passed by found himself without a tray.

When they returned, Sibelle was delighted. Her eyes gleamed when she looked upon the prince.

"Well, hello," she said.

"Prince Terren of the Realm of Toleran, glad to meet you."

"I'm Lady Sibelle, from the House of Flyn."

The prince took Sibelle's hand and brought it to his lips.

"Coming over to the dark side, eh?" Sibelle asked with a giggle.

The prince laughed. "I give all consideration."

Sibelle smiled and grabbed his arm and a flute. "Let's dance."

Prince Terren danced with Sibelle, but as soon as the dance was over, he stood in front of Orlana. "My lady? May I have this dance?"

Sibelle's face displayed a mixture of emotions: horror, surprise, and fear. "No!" she said and tried to jump in between them.

Prince Terren held out a hand towards Orlana. She reached forward and accepted. The prince whisked her onto the dance floor.

Orlana seemed to know how to dance, and soon, many in the crowd watched the beautiful couple. They stood back until the floor was wide open to them.

Orlana saw Lord Flyn and King Kheelan watching and shivered.

"What is wrong, my lady?" asked the prince.

"I cannot tell you, my lord. But I fear when this dance is over, I will have to leave."

"Then this dance cannot end."

Once dance blended into another and another, and before she knew it, Orlana was standing in front of two golden thrones: King Oberon and Queen Tania.

The prince stopped the music when they reached the king's feet. "Queen

Tania, I would be so honored if I could borrow your wand."

Now this was a very unusual request. The king stood, but somehow, Queen Tania knew that the prince's intentions were good and tossed him the wand.

The wand was very beautiful, and Orlana was in awe to be so close to something so precious. It sparkled in the evening light. It was so glittery, it seemed alive.

"I will have my servant returned to me at once!" Lord Flyn said, stepping forward.

King Kheelan dashed to grab Orlana, but it was too late. Prince Terren touched the glitter wand to Orlana's wrist, and the contained radiance burst forward. The world exploded with golden light. All the fae shielded their eyes.

"My baby, oh, my baby," Queen Tania said, hugging Orlana tightly.

"Seize them!" the king said, pointing to the two moth lords.

King Kheelan and Lord Flyn were captured and placed in confinement. Their trials would reveal who all were involved in the kidnapping of the future golden queen.

When the glitter wand tapped upon the Ring of Darkness, it shattered. Even though she was but a baby when she was abducted, all the knowledge came to her of what had happened. She looked up into Prince Terren's eyes.

"How can I ever thank you?" she asked.

"Marry me," he said, and reached down to kiss her. All the fae cheered.

After a brief courtship, Prince Terren and Princess Orlana were *married. The prophecy came true. When Orlana assumed the throne as queen, her light vanquished the moth lords to the darkest recesses of the world. All the tricks from leprechauns and dwarves ended. They, and their riches, disappeared forever.*

The moths, destined to the dark, were sad. They'd been touched by Orlana's brightness and would forever be attracted to the light.

For many years, under the rule of King Terren and Queen Orlana, the Realm of the Faeries knew peace once more.

*If you liked this story, please leave me a positive review on Amazon and Goodreads (and whereever else you'd like).   Thank you!

Sheri Chapman <3

Sheri Chapman

<u>Author Bio:</u>

Sheri Chapman loves life and laughing, but you couldn't tell it by her writing. Although she writes historical romance, a lot of her work is suspense/thriller, supernatural, shape shifter, dark fiction, and a dab of horror.

Sheri retired from teaching in Missouri Public schools with thirty years of experience in 2020. Now she splits her time between writing and working on her farmette. Sheri has chickens and a few Nigerian goats, but most of her non-writing time goes to raising exotic-colored fluffy Pomeranians.

On the personal front, Sheri is the mother of four beautiful daughters. She and their father enjoy spending time with each other, family, and friends. Aside from reading and writing, Sheri loves animals and being outdoors. She likes going for walks, fishing, scuba diving, kayaking, playing games, and watching movies. She is a big Harry Potter fan.

For those interested in Sheri's educational background, she received her bachelor's degree and first master's in special education from Missouri State University. Later, she pursued administration and got a second master's and a specialist degree from Lindenwood University in educational leadership.

Author website:
https://prayerpawpuppies.wixsite.com/authorsheric
hapman/books

www.ingramcontent.com/pod-product-compliance
Lightning Source LLC
Chambersburg PA
CBHW050819190726
48286CB00007B/1927

SHERI CHAPMAN
THE OTHER SIDE OF
Privileged

Copyright © 2021 by Trient Press

All rights reserved. No part of this publication may be reproduced, distributed, or transmitted in any form or by any means, including photocopying, recording, or other electronic or mechanical methods, without the prior written permission of the publisher, except in the case of brief quotations embodied in critical reviews and certain other noncommercial uses permitted by copyright law. For permission requests, write to the publisher, addressed "Attention: Permissions Coordinator," at the address below.

Criminal copyright infringement, including infringement without monetary gain, is investigated by the FBI and is punishable by up to five years in federal prison and a fine of $250,000.

Except for the original story material written by the author, all songs, song titles, and lyrics mentioned in the novel The Silent Wars are the exclusive property of the respective artists, songwriters, and copyright holder.

Trient Press
3375 S Rainbow Blvd
#81710, SMB 13135
Las Vegas,NV 89180

Ordering Information:
Quantity sales. Special discounts are available on quantity purchases by corporations, associations, and others. For details, contact the publisher at the address above.
Orders by U.S. trade bookstores and wholesalers. Please contact Trient Press: Tel: (775) 996-3844;   or visit www.trientpress.com.

Printed in the United States of America

Publisher's Cataloging-in-Publication data
Chapman, Sheri
A title of a book :The Other Side of Privileged

ISBN

Hardcover	978-1-955198-14-1
Paperback	978-1-955198-15-8
E-book	978-1-955198-16-5